Cattle of Kings

The First Passage

By Antonio Gully

ISBN-978-0-692-19889-6

Library of Congress Control Number 2018913388

Printed and bound in the United States of America

First Printing November 2018

Published by Antonio Gully

To order additional copies of this book, contact the author:

Antonio Gully
cattleofkings.info@gmail.com

Table of Contents

The First Passage

Preface

A place far different from the world you know today, far removed from what you consider normal. A reality no longer ruled by a single government, but by the People's Union. We knew what we wanted. We decided we would fight and die to get it. Unfortunately, that's what it took, and even more.

On the long road to create this reality, we needed our own banks, to control our money and its value. Our own insurance companies and hospitals that worked to prevent and cure, not to poison or prolong. It was now that we understood the value of all life, and every breath that came with it. We wanted our own schools to teach the truth of the past, present, and future. To equip our youths with the knowledge of the world, to create a culture that could prevail in any corner of the planet. But most importantly, teach innovation, on how to make life simple, peaceful, righteous, our own heaven on Earth, for all, and many generations to come.

UPSIDE DOWN WORLD

It was there, school, where I first met her. Aaizza (Eye-E-Zah), from the moment I saw her, I knew our bond was destiny and would last long pass our ascension. We became friends very young in grade school, when her family moved to St. Louis, MO. from Zaire. That was many years ago. Even though we graduated, we still studied together to prepare for an unknown future.

When we weren't doing community projects or work for our business, we spent time educating ourselves on the many secrets kept from our people. To lethal vaccines distributed for decades for population control, weather manipulation, black markets and much more. Most importantly, we researched the advancements needed to propel us far forward into the future.

We, sometimes, wondered what other secrets of the world awaited to be discovered. But if things went as our opposers planned, we probably wouldn't find out until many years after the damage has been done. To learn it all was like getting an entire degree in the art of manipulation, greed, and hatred. After studying, Aaizza would say, "This did nothing but add fuel to our fire to fight for what was right, the truth, for peace, for the heaven our people deserved on Earth." Though we loved to learn about the many mysteries of the generations before us and future advancements, I fell in love with Psychology and the study of the human body, while Aaizza fiend for the knowledge of the sciences and space.

It was today that I finally asked her, "What is it about science that intrigues you so much?"

She looked at me with her infamous side-eye and said, "Do you know everything about your home and those in it?"

I replied, "Yes!"

"Well, I don't," she said, as we packed up our stuff to head out of the library.

Confused, I asked, "What the hell does that have to do with science though?"

She grabbed her bag full of books and said, "Everything! It has everything to do with science! Just because you consider that shack on the Westside your home, doesn't mean the shack I stay in is anything more than a place where I occasionally lay my head to rest. She is my home, all of her!"

"She?" I replied as we walked out of the library doors.

She suddenly stopped at the top of the library steps as the shine of the Sun greeted her body, causing her to bless me with one of the only things I deemed pure, her smile. The Sun danced off her melanated skin, giving her the glow of chocolate gold. She opened her arms, as if she let the energy and light sprint through her being.

Looking into the horizon with a stare that seemed to reach the plains of Asia or the depths of the African Nile, she said, "She is, Earth, and I'm in love with her, everything about her. Her biology, her chemistry, her anatomy, her science, my home. It's straight love, you feel me?"

Gazing off into the treetops, hypnotized by the poetry of her words, I simply replied, "Word, I feel you."

"Good, 'cause she housing you and a bunch of other dirty no fucks given jokers, rent free, and y'all ain't doing nothing but messing up the creator's crib, with y'all ignorance and negligence. Clowns!" she said, walking off.

"Daaaaamn, that's how you feel though? Don't put me in the same category, I love my Earth dearly, you know that," I immediately responded, trying to catchup.

Smiling, she replied, "Yeah I know, and that's why you're my day 1."

"Yeah yeah, come at my head like that again and you gone have to see me with the hands," I said jokingly.

She laughed and replied, "You don't want these problems."

As we walked down the packed city streets, you could see the bond formed between the people. Happiness and peace of mind filled the air. Smiles roamed free as everyone greeted each other from close and afar with head nods, daps and hugs. Everywhere you turned, there was prosperity. The booming black businesses on every corner backed the people, and the people backed them. Waves of kindred spirits walked the freshly paved avenues. Newly renovated green homes equipped with enough technology to live off the grid within the city. Community patrol officers walked the streets, challenging kids to be and do their best. I used to hate to walk down these streets growing up, now I loved it. Our city came a long way and we were only going to take it further.

We continued down the street under the shadows of fruit trees that lined the curb.

The sun peeped through the leaves, shining off her fro and back as we walked toward the tracks where vendors sold and bartered goods. We always walked this way after the library, where we re'd up on materials or grabbed a snack. Like most days after the library, I was in the mood for my home girl, Zina's (Zee-na) famous Moringa, lemon, Spirulina, Seaweed, Coconut, and honey tea. It gave me energy that lasted all day. Aaizza wanted a coconut filled with pineapples, various berries, and papaya as usual.

Approaching the tracks, suddenly, both of our phones went off. We looked at each other in confusion over the odd coincidence. We grabbed our phones immediately, it was a coded message from Selah, Aaizza's father. He called for an emergency meeting, it must be serious.

Selah was the most respected man in the New St. Louis. He was one of the fathers of the paradigm shift, bringing hoods together from all corners of the city to fight for one cause, peace and prosperity for our culture. It seemed as if Selah had been working for the people his entire life. He did everything from picking up garbage to leading marches. He was a true servant leader. But to most, his biggest feat for the people was fathering one of the first of its kind, the most prestigious Montessori institutions in the country, Selassi University. But that was some time ago. Since then, Selah resigned as President of Selassi University, and was now in hiding. He had a new mission. To give the power to the people.

If you knew Selah, you'd know where Aaizza got her fire and passion for the people from. Many people loved Selah, he had the statue of a God and spoke the truth like one as well. Since the years after the rebellion, many things had changed. Many schools were now full of innovation, love, and learning. Though many also employed armed officers, homes had automatic weapons posted on the roof, and markets had to test of all foods brought or grown from outside of the New St. Louis. With the dangers of pollution increasing rapidly to toxic levels in busy cities over the years, the people of the New St. Louis collectively decided to make a change. Those willing and able traveled by foot or bike. Others used the community vehicles and other mobile electric devices. Though Aaizza and I had bikes, today, we walked, all the way to the Westside, a stent from where Selah was located.

With the tracks in sight, Aaizza said, "Yo, I love the Sun but it's way too hot for this long ass walk, let's take the shortcut after we go see Zina."

I looked at her and curled up my lips in disbelief then said, "Because you hot? You sure it's not because you know your Pops not 'bout to wait on your ass?"

"Yeah, that too, but you didn't have to say it like that though," she replied, rolling her eyes. We finally made it to the tracks, where it seemed everybody and their momma was, as usual.

Growing up, the Hodiamont Tracks wasn't the place for walking. But now, in today's world, many people use it to sell and trade goods out of their backyards or carts. Some called it the Barabara Watu (Bah-ra-bah-ra Wah-too), which meant "The People's Highway". It was the massive amount of people that filled the track on a daily basis, that's what earned its name. The tracks, as usual, was full of life with people trying to prosper and serve the culture. This was one of the many places here in the city where locals would go get everything from fresh foods, counseling, pets, clothes, to literature, and even medicine. As we made it through the thick crowd, dodging bikes riders, hoverboards, skateboarders and other mobile contraptions, we finally made it to Zina's yard where she was under the tent making some new brew. Zina and her family had the purest herbs, teas, and natural medicines on the tracks.

"Hey girl! What you over there brewing up this time?" Aaizza yelled, entering the yard.

Zina looked up and said, "Aaz! Girl you know I can't tell you about my brews, if I do I have to kill you."

"Shit, I hope it's something for those crusty ass feet," I said under my breath. Aaizza laughed.

Clearly hearing what I said, Zina rolled her eyes and said, "Syr (Si-year) (But everyone just called me Sir), you always got some slick shit to say, huh! I don't say nothing about y'all needing a liter of aloe gel to moisturize those ashy ass locs! Walking around like you got cradle cap!"

"Dang, I can't laugh?!" Aaizza said, grinning.

"Nah, you can't! But anyway, what's up though? What y'all doing in my neck of the woods, besides bothering folks?" Zina said.

"Let us get the usual sis, we're on our way to a meeting with Selah, so you know we need as much energy as possible!" Aaizza said.

"Yes girl, I know. Syr, go grab that bag behind those plants over there for me please," Zina said, pointing to a bag ducked off in the corner.

I immediately headed toward the bag, making my way through the assortment of crystals, plants, spices, fruits, and other shit she either grew or made. As I navigated through her creations, I could hear Aaizza whisper, "Is my hair really that ashy though girl? Let me get a bottle of the aloe gel too."

I grabbed the bag of ingredients, then walked back to where they were waiting. Zina grabbed the bag and got to work, whipping up our healthy concoctions. Though little time had passed, I reminded her that we should be leaving soon. The last thing I wanted was Selah coming at my head for lacking urgency. As soon as I finished reminding Aaizza of the time, Zina was handing us our drinks, and a bottle of aloe gel.

"What do we owe sis?" I said.

"The usual, just come by next week and help me get this garden together, I'm going to need y'all muscles, Azzi maybe you can finally help me make some jewelry!" Zina suggested.

Like most people now, we traded goods for goods, or for favors, but because she was the homie, we probably would've done it for free.

"If y'all are done with the king in time, we should meet up at the Friday Fights. It should be good this week I heard," Zina added.

"Yea, I heard that too! Hopefully, this won't take long. But we are talking about Selah, so who knows. Well, let us make this move sista, we're already running late," Aaizza said.

"Ok, get going! Peace, love, and prosperity," Zina said as we headed out the yard.

We replied with the same.

Heading back down the tracks, we cut through colorful backyards and vacant lots filled with gardens of vegetables of all kinds. Some of the gardens rested in glass houses, while others were uniquely placed around homes and structures.

While enjoying her drink, Azzi randomly said, "I love nature. But me and flowers, have a love-hate relationship. Like I hate roses. Well, not hate, just strongly dislike them. Especially the white ones. I don't know why. But what I do hate is when someone cuts them, kills them, then gives them to me wrapped in plastic and paper. If you ever want to give me flowers, don't. You'll make me happier by leaving it where the Creator planted it."

"Really?! Well, that makes a lot of sense," I responded, thinking if I ever gave her flowers in the past. I could only think of one joker that did.

We walked until we entered a heavily-wooded park that was a shortcut to Selah's current location. He always moved around because of threats on his life and freedom, like many of the others that grew up in his time. Though Selah was in hiding, working to secure a prosperous future for his people, he still remained a father. Azzi is all he has, so he made sure she was set after he left. Having something happen to her is one of his biggest fears, and rightfully so. She was his only child, if anything was to happen to him, she would take over everything and replace Selah. At a young age, he gave me the job to watch over her, protect her, and since then, I've done just that, she is all he has, and in a way, she's all I have as well.

Making our way through the park of various trees, we approached an opening where the light from the sun shinned deep into the wooded area. Exposing fruits that glew like rubies on the trees. We absorbed the beauty of nature around us. I could see Azzi falling in love with 'Her' all over again. As we marveled at the majestic sight produced by nature, I could see the swaying fields of glowing vegetation off in the distance. We walked toward the sunshine. Stepping out of the wooded area, we were greeted by fields and fields of tall vivid green Hemp stalks dancing in the wind. The harmony and unison, reminded me of my connection with the

Earth, the Creator, and my people. It was beautiful. Stalks with buds like small pine trees, bedded by long green feathers, bobbed from side to side, like the breeze was playing its favorite song. Feeling one with the Earth, our energy joined and bobbed to the tunes as well.

Navigating the path through the Hemp fields, enjoying our goods, she turned with a look of confusion and mild worry, then said, "What you think he wants to tell us, Syr?"

Knowing that it may be more serious, I simply replied, "He probably just wants to check on you like always, maybe update us, who knows?"

"There are ways to do that without all of this walking," she complained. "Well, we're almost there. You'll find out soon enough, with yo ol' scary ass," I said to lighten the situation and ease her mind.

"You right, and the only thing scary is your face while you talking," she replied as we tracked through the thick brush of crops.

As usual, I didn't have a comeback, so I just shut up and tried to think of one. It seemed like all the good ones came to me hours after the joke was over. I hated that shit.

We were getting close to our destination. Clearing the trees and heavy vegetation, we could see a secluded home off in the cut. Walking up to the large Westside brick house right on time. Aaizza did her token knock that hasn't changed since we were little. We instantly heard an uproar of dog barks. As we patiently waited, we could hear his heavy footsteps walking towards the door.

"Easy," a deep voice said, abruptly silencing the guard dogs.

As he opened the door, you could see the Sun revealing his 6'8 linebacker statue. He looked down on us with a stern mug and said, "Get in here."

The first thing that came to mind was, "Aww shit, this Negus mad."

As we walked passed and greeted the 7 Tibian Mastiff, Ovcharka, and Gull Dong mix guard dogs standing at attention, I couldn't help but notice the extra weight they've put on. Clearly, all of them where over 200 pounds now and barely over a year old.

"Damn, they've gotten so big," I whispered to Aaizza.

"Yea big and crazy," she replied.

Following Selah, we could hear the voices of several men as we approached the door of a room. Selah stopped and turned to Aaizza, then grabbed her by the hands. "Sorry for my sternness. "Are you peaceful, my Princess?" he asked.

"I am as always. Are you peaceful, father?" she replied.

"Today, I don't know love, but we shall see soon enough. Peace Syr, what's good?" he then turned to me and said.

Awaiting anxiously to enter the room to find out the news, I answered, "Peace Family, I guess we are about to see."

"You're right. Follow me," Selah said, opening the door to the room.

As we walked into the large, dimly lit room, all conversation halted, as to resume where Selah left-off.

I greeted, "Peace Gods" as I gazed around the room filled with soldiers and generals from all over the city.

Ducked off into the corner, I saw my brother, Kano. Over the years, he earned the name for being a wild card, and never taking a 'L', for nobody. I suddenly realized something very serious was going down.

After Aaizza greeted the room, she curiously turned to Selah and asked, "What's going on? Why is everyone here? This many people shouldn't know!"

"Sit down," Selah replied.

As he looked upon the room of battle-ready hue'd men, Selah took a deep breath and said, "We have been notified of a pending attack here in the city, today!"

My breath left my body. An eerie silence filled the room with looks of disgust, rage, and fear. You could hear the heartbeat of the room go from the sound of steady footsteps of a tall man on wood floors to a furious beat of an African drum. It was at that moment, I knew shit just got real.

"One of our informants alerted us recently but didn't tell us where or by who!" Selah finished.

"Those mafuckas! I bet it's the White Knights!" One general said.

"No! I bet it's the Government!" said another.

"Who are our enemies?! We have to go to the source!" another general argued.

"Enemies? Nigga, half the world has been trained hate niggas! Even some niggas hate niggas! No telling who can be attacking today! We need to be focusing on getting our people indoors!" Kano said from deep in the corner.

"The schools let out early today, so where could it be?" a general asked.

"No services at the Mosque or Church?" another general said.

"The fights?!" I suggested.

"Yea, everybody will be there, we were going when we left here," Aaizza added.

Selah instantly said, "Strap up, and get everyone together, get our people out of there now!"

Everybody stood up and frantically headed for the door. Everybody rushed out of the door with their phones, calling and texting coded messages to alert the soldiers and people they knew were headed to the fights.

"Call Zina!" Aaizza said with urgency.

I called but it went straight to voicemail. I called again, only to get the same. This time, I left a message. "Don't go to the fights! Stay yo ass at home! Spread the word. Call me back ASAP."

Aaizza and I headed for the door to go alert the people. That's when Selah grabbed Aaizza and said, "Where the fuck, do you think you're going? Sit down, I can't let you be a part of this madness! You could be a target!"

Aaizza turned with the look of a mad dog being held by its tail and said, "Sit down?! Our people have done enough sitting down, backing down, only to be let down! That shit dead, I will not sit down and watch my people die by the hands of peons. These clowns want G shit? Well, I'ma give it to em." She snatched her arm away and walked out of the door.

"Damn it! Kano, go with her!" Selah ordered.

As I turned to follow them, Selah said in a fatherly tone, "Syr, protect my princess."

I replied, "Selah, she's all of our Princess, I'll protect her with my life."

I ran out of the door to catch up with Kano and Aaizza on their way to Kano s car parked in the lot hidden by vegetation. "Y'all strapped?" Kano asked as he went to open the trunk of his old school Chevelle.

"No, we just left the library!" I replied.

"The fuck?! What does that mean? Nigga we are in the middle of a war! And we're still behind enemy lines! Books don't block bullets. Both of y'all need to tighten up! Here!" Kano said, sternly popping the trunk, revealing an arsenal of deadly weaponry.

Aaizza didn't waste any time picking up the mini AR15 and a 38. I grabbed the choppa. Kano looked at me and said, "Nah, I think this one is a little more appropriate for this occasion." He then handed me a fully auto shotgun with the Mickey Mouse ears. It looked like something off a video game, but unfortunately, due to the current state of our society, seeing this had become normal.

We skirted off into the fleet of trucks armed to the teeth, headed to the fights on the other side of town. We called Zina again, no answer. Just an eerie silence filled the speeding car, showing everyone was in deep thought, about how our lives would change in the next few minutes. Though she had a look of cold iron on her face, I knew she was scared, holding her weapon like a master samurai with his sword preparing for battle. Kano was cool, this shit wasn't new to him. After being locked up for a decade, ain't no telling what type of shit he's done or is willing to do in the name of the culture. He didn't care, he was a seasoned soldier and the best soldier. Though I was trained in combat, as was many of the men in our culture now, I knew this wasn't the way of life we wanted, we wanted peace and happiness. As we sped through lights, flying pass cars and pedestrians, with the roar of his 454 elderbrock, and the beat of old Wu-Tang Clan, "It could all be so simple," I could feel the anxiety building as we got closer. Aaizza began to check her AR, I did the same, making sure it wouldn't jam in the midst of battle.

Coming up to the block of the Fights, we could see the other members of the Calvary pulling up and getting out. Someone sounded the alarm for people to take cover and get ready for a potential threat. As the alarm rang through the park, people scattered frantically, looking for cover. Neighborhood churches and safe houses filled rapidly. Kano pulled up on the grass of the park and we jumped out. Aaizza and I headed to find Zina, while Kano went the other direction. We fought our way through the stampede of people, looking for our friend. People held the look of fear as heavily armed soldiers circulated through the crowd, warning people to get home. It was too packed. Thousands in attendance. There was no way to get everyone to safety in time. I followed Aaizza to the hill where Zina's family had a cart and sold her goods at every fight, but it was simply too crowded to get there. Fed up, I lifted shotgun in the air and squeezed the trigger! I only pulled the trigger once and 4 shots went off with the thunderous sound of dynamite. BOOM! BOOM! BOOM! BOOM! It cleared the park as people ran frantically. The streets filled with cars and people searching for safety. We didn't know if it would be a bomb or mass shooting, either way, our people shouldn't be there to find out.

Aaizza screamed, "There!" She spotted Zina running for cover across the street.

We called and finally caught up to her. "Zina! Zina!" Aaizza yelled.

She stopped and turned around. "Azzi! What the fuck is going on?! Why y'all got those guns?!" she yelled.

"There was a threat of an attack today! We need to get everybody out of here now!" Aaizza replied.

Suddenly, another drumroll of an automatic weapon rang through the park! We hid behind a car, where I pumped the shotty and Aaizza cocked the AR. We looked at each other, bracing ourselves for the ensuing gun battle. Armed and ready, we started back across the street to the park. Creeping and looking through the aim of my weapon, feeling like I was in a game of Call of Duty. Out of nowhere, I heard the sound of tires coming to a screeching halt. We cautiously dove in the grass and lifted our guns, ready to fire! It was Kano! "Get in!" he yelled, opening the door.

We ran to the car and got in, Zina came out of hiding and jumped in too. As we sped off, barely having time to close the door, Kano began to beat the steering wheel. "It was a set up, they fucking set us up!" he yelled in anger.

"What the hell is going on!" I asked with my stomach turning in fear of the news he was about to drop on us.

"Selah hit the alarm beacon, the house is under attack! That park attack shit was phony bro! We have to get back to save him!" he said in anger as he weaved recklessly through the crowd of running people and dodging traffic back to the Westside.

With her head buried in her lap, Aaizza uttered with a cracking voice, "This must stop, this must stop now!"

Zina consoled her in the backseat. With tears in her eyes, Zina said to Kano, "You have a gun for me?"

"Look under the seat," he replied.

Under the seat, she found a loaded 45. Finally turning the corner to Selah's current hideout, we were greeted with gun fire that riddled the hood of the car. The bodies of some of the intruders and Selah guards laid in the yard, some dead, all wounded. The dogs where ripping 3 of the intruders to pieces in the bushes. Looking up, we saw Selah being forced at gun point into one of the two vehicles.

"Look!! They have my father!" Aaizza screamed, instantly sticking her gun out of the window and opening fire at the cars of the kidnappers. The men fired back as they sped off with Selah captive in the car. We followed, firing at will.

"Aim for the tires!" Kano said as we raced through the Westside in hot pursuit.

We got closer as the torque of the old school engine burned rubber every time we switched gears. We fired at the tires every chance we got, hoping not to hit the very man we were trying to save. Suddenly, the car in front turned down a side street, splitting away from the car that held Selah. We continued to follow the car that held Selah, allowing the other car to get away.

Nearing the edge of the city limits, I yelled, "Fishtail his ass, Kano!" remembering the maneuver from an old episode of Cops.

Kano Slammed on the gas and rammed the backside of the car, making it lose control and crash into a solar pole. We instantly jumped out with our weapons drawn. Kano ran to the driver's door and fired two shots into the head of the driver, to insure there was no escape. With the windows shattered, we could see the front passenger knocked out from the impact of the crash. The other two men that sat in the back guarding Selah, were starting to come back to reality. Realizing they were waking up, Kano opened the back door and gun butted one while the rest of us held the other at gunpoint. Selah, was slumped in the middle, not moving.

Aaizza called out to him, "Daddy!"

THE SUN SETS ON A KING

We all sat there, silently awaiting a response from our King.

Aaizza called him again, "Father!" There was still no response.

Kano snatched one of the masked kidnappers out of the car. Aaizza immediately jumped in to try to get a response out of the lifeless body of her father. He didn't budge. Zina began to cry as if she knew what this meant.

Then suddenly, Selah lifted his head, face covered in blood, cracked a crooked smile and mumbled to Aaizza, "My baby, you out here saving folks in shit. I guess you're my hero now." Aaizza embraced her father and wiped the blood from his face.

As Aaizza and Zina helped him out of the car slowly, Kano walked up and threw me some rope and duct tape. "Bro, help me get these clowns out the car and tie them up! We don't have much time!" Kano said.

I quickly snatched another guy out the car and kneed him in the mouth. Kano grabbed the last guy, then did the same. By now, the Queens had Selah secured in the car. We hurried and hogged tied the savages then stuffed them in the trunk. Squirming like fish in a bucket, we gun butted them a few more times just to tenderize them a little.

Out of breath, Kano said, "Welcome, you have just been enrolled into Trunk University. We have a 100% graduation rate, to the afterlife! Class starts now!" then he slammed the trunk.

As we hurried and jumped into the car, I said, "I wonder how long you been waiting to say that crazy shit."

"You'll be surprised! I thought it was pretty clever actually," he mumbled back to me as he started the car and sped off back into the city.

"Hurry, he's losing a lot of blood!" Aaizza screamed.

Zina began tightening the tied shirts she found under the seat around his wounds to slow the leak. "We need to take him to the hospital now!" Zina pleaded.

With her face covered in tears and sweat, Aaizza held her father closely, rubbing her fingers through his grey locs.

"No, take me to the house on Clemens! Across from the vacant school. I'm going to be fine. Alert the doc and tell him to meet us there," Selah uttered in his deep powerful voice, reassuring everything will be ok.

The house on Clemens was another hideout that only few knew about. Aaizza and I didn't even know exactly where it was located,

Kano did though. We couldn't go back to the Westside after what just happened there. We were sure the car that got away was going to come back with backup, searching for their butt buddies.

So, we hurried towards the new hideout on Clemens Street, to get Selah out of danger, and to medical attention immediately. As we blazed frantically through the side streets, I could feel the tension and fear in the car.

That's when Aaizza asked, "Who are these guys that attacked the house and tried to kidnap you? Do you know?"

"I'm not sure, but they're professionals. We didn't even see them coming. During the attack, I snatched a life-like mask of a black man off of a white face. They could be anybody," Selah responded.

"Don't worry about that, we will find out soon enough. Ain't that right?!" Kano yelled to the trunk. He then turned to Selah and said, "Hang in there, we're almost there."

When we arrived at the house, Kano drove through some fake bushes and parked in a secluded part of this huge backyard. The Doc was already there, waiting. He rushed to the car and helped us carry Selah into the house. Once inside, the Doc began working to stop the bleeding and patching him up in a room in the back. Though Selah was doing better and looking like he was going to make it, Aaizza still held a look of anguish. I could see this situation eating away at her once peaceful pure being. I could only imagine how she felt, it was her father. The most consistent and positive person in her life. Kano and I couldn't fathom such a feeling. Not knowing what to say, I grabbed her hand and pulled her close. She embraced me firmly and buried her head in my chest.

I rubbed my hands through her silky rich fro and told her, "I am here for you, forever, and I mean that shit, Azzi." And I did, I meant every word. I hugged her tight, hoping to steal some of her grief to replace it with love and security.

I wiped the tears from her eyes, as she looked at me and replied, "I know, and you've always been there. That's why you my Negus." Locking eyes, we smiled at each other.

That's when Kano tapped me on my shoulder, "Help me grab these clowns out the trunk," he said, walking towards the door. Aaizza released me and I followed Kano out the door.

"So, what are we going to do with them?" I asked as I trailed behind through the big backyard.

"Well, that depends on how much they feel like talking. We need to know who sent them, and what other shit they may have up their sleeve. With that being said, it's going to be a long night, bro. Pop the trunk!" Kano replied.

As we stood next to the car, we could hear them moving. I got my gun ready just in case one of the men got loose. I opened the trunk to see them covered in blood and gasping for air. Kano gun butted the first one and snatched him out of the trunk. I did the same thing and grabbed another. We dragged them to the basement. I then went back to the trunk to grab the last hogtied punk.

Now that the men were in the house, blindfolded, gaged, and locked in the basement, Kano and I went upstairs to ask Selah what to do next. Now sitting up on the bed, with all of the blood cleaned off his face and drinking a glass of water, we could see he was doing much better.

We walked in and Kano said, "they're downstairs, what do you want us to do next?"

Selah stood, towering over everyone in the house, almost casting a shadow over the room. He took a deep breath, seeming to reset his mind and releasing his physical pain. He spoke, "Aaizza, go look behind the refrigerator and grab that black bag and bring it here."

She hurried out of the room to grab the bag and handed it to Selah.

"Y'all follow me, you too Doc," Selah said as he walked to the basement, and slowly started down the stairs. We followed.

Aaizza grabbed Kano, "What's going on? What's about to happen?" she said.

Kano grinned like the Chestshire Cat, revealing his mouth full of gold teeth then whispered in her ear, "These Bacon boys 'bout to talk or it's time to take the pigs to the slaughter house. You like barbeque, right?"

"No, I'm Vegan. Wait what? No!" Aaizza said then raced down the steps to stop Selah.

Kano laughed. She ran in front of him and screamed, "No Father! We can't harm them!"

"And why the hell not Aaizza? These savages tried to kidnap me! They killed many of our men! Those men were fathers, brothers, sons, and there's no telling what they would've done to me if you all weren't there to save me. We need answers! We must act now or find ourselves in this position again. Now, let me handle this!" Selah said sternly.

Standing next to the steps still grinning, Kano chimed in and said, "I'm sorry but I'm confused, what happened to all that tough G shit you spoke of earlier?"

Aaizza rolled her eyes at Kano, looked back at Selah and said, "Daddy, this makes us no better them. It was you that taught me that violence is the lowest form of communication. It was you that said that."

Selah put down the bag and said, "We didn't hunt them, they hunted us, we don't hate them, they hate us! But now, the rabbit has caught the fox red handed. If we let him go, he'll be back, and next time, we may not be this lucky." He picked the bag up and walked away and told Kano and I to come with him, then ordered Doc to watch the ladies as he entered the room.

Zina walked to Aaizza and told her, "We've played enough defense, it's time to play some 'O' Sista, Phil Jackson style."

Aaizza fed all of us some side-eye then walked upstairs, Zina and the Doc followed. I walked in the room where we were keeping our estranged guests, then closed the door.

Once in the room, Selah ordered Kano and I to take the hoods off their heads. Now all awake, we could see the fear in their eyes behind all the blood on their faces. Shaking, distraught, and oblivious to where they were, they began to spew out muffled screams. But to no avail. We sat calmly, just watching them squirm, scream, and plea.

Fed up with the noise, Selah, in a deep, relaxed tone said, "Please, your screams, your cries, go on deaf ears and merciless hearts. If you like, we can give you ample reason to scream and to cry."

They quickly simmered down. Selah pulled up a stool and asked the now quiet murderous kidnapers, "So, who wants to go first? Who sent you?"

There was no response, just silence and nervous stares.

Selah giggled a little and said, "Oh, don't you all speak at once!" He laughed a little more, then stood up to open the black bag. He first, pulled out a pair of black latex gloves and put them on. He threw a pair to Kano and I.

"Put those on," he said. Next, he pulled out a blender, a funnel, glasses, a bottle of 151, and an old dusty bottle of Hennessy Black that looked like it had been aging since I was born. He blessed the bottle then cracked it open.

He turned to us and said, "Thirsty?" then poured 3 drinks.

Kano obliged and said, "I don't mind if I do," as he took his drink and handed me mine.

I was confused as hell, almost as confused as the ass monkeys tied up and stuffed in the corner. I sat back and thought, *Selah had us do all this just to get everybody drunk? Hell, he has a full bar in that bag.*

I turned to Kano and whispered, "What is dude doing?"

Kano just grinned and said, "Just chill and have your drink. This is going to get good."

I looked back at Selah as he dug back in the bag and pulled out some lock cutters, an adrenalin needle, pliers, and a machete. He then turned to me and told me to put some coals in the furnace and start it up. Before I did, I took a drink of the melanated beverage Selah poured for me. Feeling the burn of the drink all the way to me stomach, I cringed a little, then whipped my mouth with my shirt sleeve. Hoping nobody saw my reaction to the stiff drink, I hurried to grab the shovel, add coals, and start the furnace. Once the flames got started, Selah grabbed the bottle and funnel then sat in front of the tied-up men.

"So, who needs a drink?" he asked, looking around at the men. "You! You look like you need a drink. Kano remove his gag," Selah said, pointing to the guy on the end. Kano put down his drink and snatched the gag out of the mouth of the first guy.

Selah wore this very inviting smile, which was extremely creepy considering the situation. He asked, still smiling, "What's y'all names, Lil mella?"

"Darren, George, and Ron," he replied in a mumble with his head down.

Holding the bottle and funnel, Selah asked, "So Darren, you tryna hit this bottle or nah?"

Sensing his current predicament and the tension in the room, Darren realized it was going to be a long night and reluctantly nodded his head yes.

Laughing, Selah replied, "Yeah, I think we all need one, especially after today."

He then leaned over and put the funnel in Darren's mouth, then poured a nice size shot of 151 down the funnel. Darren snatched his head away from the funnel and cringed. His face twisted up as residue from the shot ran down his chin. The hideous reaction of his face made us laugh.

"Boooi you ugglass shit!" Kano said, laughing and looking at Darren.

"Damn, you good?" Selah asked, grinning in amusement.

Darren replied with a nod.

Selah stopped laughing abruptly and said, "Now tell me who sent you." There was a short awkward silence, then Selah continued,

"Let me guess, you're with the KKK, White Knights, Nazi, Cointel Pro, some random rural militia that knows none but hates all blacks? Shit the government? Tell us something, we don't have time to go through the phone book list of hate groups your kind has created."

Darren remained silent, looking around to avoid eye contact.

Selah sat back in his chair with a cold hard stare and said, "Look at me, look…at …me. We can do this the easy way, or the hard way, the choice is yours."

I instantly took a sip of my drink, realizing how real shit just got for him. Although I secretly hoped he just spilled the beans, Darren didn't budge. He didn't make a sound, he just kept his big ass head down. I couldn't blame him, because I would've done the same thing, if it was me, but it wasn't me. Being on the other side made me realize how dumb that silence was.

Selah stood up slowly, then walked over to his black bag and put on a black apron.

Kano looked at me and said, "Damn, that's only the first question. Bro, the haze is about to be so trill for these ass monkeys."

I just sat back and prepared myself for what was next. Sharpening the large machete he pulled out of his bag, Selah turned to me and said, "Syr, gag em, Kano cut up the radio."

I put my drink down and grabbed Darren by the extra meat folded on the back of his big bald ass head and gagged him as he tried to resist. Darren began to shake and cry. I could tell deep down, he wasn't about this life. Just another uneducated cannon fire that knew nothing about the world outside of his small, privileged, hate-filled bubble. Selah pointed at me to hold Darren's leg. Kano cut up the radio, blasting Mobb Deep's track, Survival of the Fittest. Once I grabbed his leg, Darren began to squirm, so I punched him in the meat rolls on the back of his neck to make him stop. Selah walked towards us with the machete in his hand, then grabbed Darren's ankle. Selah loaded up to swing, pulling the machete far above his head. I could feel Darren's body tense up to a stiff lock. That's when he screamed! And though he was gagged, we heard it clear over the music.

Selah stood up and snatched the gag out of his mouth and said, "You got something to tell me boy!?"

Kano turned down the music. Darren's heart was beating out of his back, crying, he said, "It was our idea, we've been planning this for months, nobody sent us, we sent ourselves!"

Selah lowered his swing, "Hmmm, is that right?" he said.

Selah then walked over to the next guy and pulled out his gag. "And what's your name?" Selah asked.

"George," he replied, looking around the room, settling his sights on his hysterical partner.

Selah kneeled in front of George, and uttered, "So Georgie, is your man telling the truth?"

George nodded his head yes.

"And that's your word, huh?" Selah said, standing up. He looked at me then Kano and said, "What y'all think?"

Kano abruptly replied, "I smell bullshit, that story stinks."

Before I could answer, not that I had an answer, Selah walked over to George, grabbed him by the neck then said, "Since you just ate that bullshit he tried to feed us, let's see if your mans will eat…you."

He then gaged George and turned him face to face with Darren. Selah grabbed George's leg by the ankle and chopped off his foot! Eyes filled with tears, George screamed to the top of his lungs as the blood from his leg began to puddle.

"Darren, look at your butt buddy! Mafucka I said look at him! Right in the eyes punk!" Selah said, walking towards his black bag with George's foot in hand. He grabbed the blender and plugged it up. "Kano, stop the bleeding, Syr hold that neck and make sure he's looking right in his eyes," Selah said.

Kano put the shovel in the furnace until it was red hot. I grabbed Darren's neck and made him look in his friend's eyes as he cried for mercy. Selah put George's foot in the blender, then cut it until his foot was soup. The sound of the shattering bones and mangled flesh was disturbing. He then added some 151. The liquid reeked of unknown odors. It looked so disgusting. Kano pulled the shovel out of the furnace slowly, the iron was red. Kano walked over to George and said, "Yo! We can't have you bleeding all over the place dying in shit. This should help." Kano pressed the shovel against the wound firmly, you could smell the flesh cooking. As George screamed and begged for mercy, I held Darren's face straight, so he could see the pain in George's eyes and the agony that filled his body.

Selah walked over to Darren with the funnel and the foot soup in the blender. He grabbed him by the jawbone and stuffed the funnel in his mouth, then poured it all down his throat. Blood, skin, toe nails, and all. I mean, I heard stories, but never would've guessed they got down like this. I could tell from the smirk of being entertained, it was obvious, this wasn't Kano s first time. Just the smell alone made me gag, I couldn't imagine having my homies' foot soup forced down my throat.

Selah emptied the blender in Darren's mouth, looked into his eyes and said, "Feed us bullshit, we feed you George. Haha, take a wild guess what's next on the menu?! Now tell me who sent you."

Still coughing from the foot slushy that he was just force-fed, Darren began to pee on himself. I instantly jumped up when some got on my shoes. Selah began to laugh but it quickly turned into a horse cough. When I turned to see what was wrong, I could see the blood coming through the bandages and his shirt. I ran to him, his hands were covered in blood after covering his cough. Noticing something was wrong, Selah sat down and I told Kano to go get the Doc. I wiped the blood from his mouth and put my hand over the bandaged wound to slow the bleeding.

I looked to him and asked, "Are you good, brother? I know this lil boo boo isn't getting the best of you!"

He smiled and replied, "Nah, I'm good brother, I just never thought this would be life, this would be our existence, forever fighting on the defense, for our right to be on this Earth, oppressed simply because of our melanin. They hate it so much, and it almost took me a lifetime to figure out why. One day, you will figure out too."

Before I could ask what it was, Kano came back with The Doc. Azzi and Zina followed behind. I moved out of the way, so they could help him.

Selah quickly said, "I'm OK. I just need to rest," as The Doc checked his wounds. Selah stood up, then called Kano. He told him, "You know what to do, if they talk, let them live. I'll be close."

As Selah walked out of the door with the assistance of The Doc and Zina, Azzi doubled back. She looked around at the 3 men and could instantly sense the barbaric temperature of the room. Blood, body parts, confusion, and pride filled the muggy dark basement. I could only imagine what was going through her head. She just looked at me and rolled her eyes, then left.

Kano closed the door then said, "Let's finish this, bro."

I turned to the hostages, grabbed the machete and said, "Now, let's not make this hard, we don't want to take your lives, because unlike you, we know every life in the eyes of the creator is a precious one and deserves the right to have the opportunity to live in heaven on Earth. But see time and time again, you prove you lack the humanity, the intellect, the peace, the respect for my people to let them live, and thrive in happiness. It's for that reason, if you do not tell me what I want to know, I will gladly snatch the savage souls out of your worthless vessels and send them to the hell from which they came. So, I'm going to ask you one last time Darren and company, who sent you?"

Kano pulled the shovel out of the furnace, Darren looked up at his friends tied up, then took a deep breath and uttered softly, "I am the leader, I convinced them to come with me."

Kano looked at me, then with a burst of anger, swung the red-hot shovel, hitting George in the back repeatedly. Furious blow after furious blow. The hot shovel melted his skin, peeling it off with every blow. Blood splattered everywhere, the intense screech of a grown man screams of agony rang through the house. Quickly, the hot metal began to expose bone. Darren stared deep in the eyes of his friend, inching closer and closer to death with every wet thud, until George faded out of consciousness.

"Ok!! Please!! Stop! We're from the M.A.H.A!" Darren reluctantly screamed. Out of breath, Kano stopped swinging and said, "What you say punk?!"

"We're from the M.A.H.A, our mission was to kidnap Selah for interrogation!" Darren yelled in reply.

Kano slammed the hot shovel against his back again and said, "Interrogation for what Pussy?!"

"To learn how to infiltrate the orgs, dismantle the unions, halt the barter currency trade, and stop the clean energy movement! Now please stop hitting him! He's going to die!" Darren said unwillingly.

"I'll think about it! Now tell me why would y'all want to sabotage something that's beneficial to all?!" I said in disbelief.

"Not all, not those in power. Ours included. Entire nations and industries here and abroad have been built on black ignorance and sweat. Now he's attempting to take that away. From enemies and allies Blacks didn't even know they had. This movement doesn't just affect the US anymore, Selah is trying to restructure the world economy. This is bigger than your skin color!" Darren replied with his head down.

"Oh, I see, they believe Black and Brown empowerment and prosperity means death and dysfunction for everyone else. Pssh, on God y'all stay on some scary shit. Fear is at the root of just about everything y'all do and create. Now y'all feel the heat from the bottom you made. But aye, we did it, and made it look good. I'm sure you and your people can manage." Kano chuckled and shook his head, then put down the shovel and grabbed his drink.

"It's not that simple! You're taking away the very thing that drives the economy! The working class!" Darren pleaded.

"Man whatever! Tell me, who is the clown that got away? What's the dude's name?" Kano asked.

"Dylan, he was the captain of the mission," Darren answered.

Still slowly sipping his drink, Kano said, "Oh really, well, isn't he a slippery one. How about you inform me of what Dylan and the M.A.H.A have planned next for us?"

That's when the last guy on the floor began to shake, and mumble under his gag. "Hell, wrong with this clown? Ungag him, he might have something to say," Kano implied.

I took the gag out, to reveal a hideous red mug with a diabolical set of oddly placed teeth. He instantly began spitting out blood from his tussle with us earlier.

He looked around the room and fixed his eyes on Darren. "You rat muthafucka, fuck them, you bet not say another fuckin word I swear!" He then turned to us and continued in the same strong Boston accent, "The fuck I suppose to be scared of you niggers and your lil movement?! It will do nothing but create an even lazier more entitled lower class! You'll be killing each other again in no time. And that ape Selah, we knew he was alive this entire time! Who do you think you are? We probably know more about him than you do. Dumbasses!"

"You're going to get us all killed you dumbass!" Darren screamed.

"No, you're the dumbass if you ever thought they were going to let us see their faces then walk out of here?! We're already dead men! These animals aren't that stupid! Like we're not stupid enough to let that traitor live! How long did you think he was going to last after that night?" he said with an evil smirk.

Kano and I turned and looked at each other in awe. "We should've kept the gag and hood on your ugly ass," I said, sipping my drink.

Then I remembered something Selah said some time back about having friends on both sides. I wondered if they got wind of Selah's inside man. Kano began to walk over to the machete, but that's when The Doc opened the door. "Come into the other room immediately!" he urged us. Kano and I gagged everyone and walked out to see what the issue was.

When I came out of the room, I could see the tears of Zina falling freely from her bloodshot eyes. As I looked at Azzi with her head down, I saw a tear trickle from her eyes like a diamond falling from the sky, leaving its home in the heavens. I could feel my stomach knotting up with emotion.

The Doc got our attention and said, "King Selah now rest in the Essence."

Lumps filled my throat, seemingly to mute the pain and rage that was building up inside. I instantly ran over to Azzi and held her tight. I wanted to say something to ease the pain, but I couldn't even ease my own, and I know she could tell. She looked at me with tears and anger filling her piercing brown eyes.

She oddly spoke with a calm tone, "He passed peacefully. He would want us to be strong."

With her delicate touch holding me tightly, her hands squeezed my shirt. She lifted her head off my chest and we gazed deeply into each other's eyes, not a word was said but her soul and heart spoke to me. We knew that in this life and after, that we will forever be there for one another. It was at that moment I felt okay and secure.

I realized she's just not the strength I need, but she's the strength the entire culture needs.

I knelt on one knee, never taking my eyes off her and said, "Goddess of Earth, Creator of Life, I am here to cherish, to protect, to serve you, until the Sun is no longer a blaze, you are my Queen."

She ran her hands through my hair while looking into my eyes. "My father will rest easy knowing you're here with me, he nor I would have it any other way."

That's when I felt a hand on my shoulder, snapping me out of a daze. It was Zina and Kano. They all got down on their knees with me.

Kano looked at us and said, "We're all in this together. We are our sister's keepers."

Zina then embraced us and said, "We are our brother's keepers."

At that moment, I realized this was only the beginning, but they were going to be there to the end. We all embraced each other, but after only a moment, Kano broke the silence, "So Queen, what you want us to do with the punks that killed Selah?"

Azzi looked up and said, "Take me to them."

We got up and walked into the room where the gagged men laid helplessly tied up on the floor. You could feel the tension in the room. The anger that filled our hearts was visible.

That's when Ron looked up, I instantly noticed that his gag was out, that's when he cracked this crooked ass grin then said, "You cock suckers make me sick. You think you're all high and mighty! Calling yourself the original man like that actually means something. You'd think since your ancestors were warriors and geniuses, they created this and that, that you muthafuckers would be tougher! I mean you call us cave dwellers but what does that make you pieces of shit?! You got ran out of your own land. Now we own you!"

"You don't own shit! See that's yall problem now, greed, envy, and fear!" I replied quickly.

"Yea see the Jews and Asians have their traditions. Italians have their families and the church. Even we have our culture and music. Ron, what the fuck do your people have?" Kano asked.

Ron looked up and replied, "We have the United States. The rest of you motherfuckers are just visiting."

"Wham!" Kano punched him in the mouth, temporarily knocking him out, and gagged him again. He stood up and looked around and said, "And look what yall did to the place." He then turned to us and added, "Oh my b, y'all weren't tryna listen to that shit, were you?"

Azzi replied, "No worries, he'll have plenty of space to express his feelings as soon as he wakes."

That's when we heard the door to the room close. We turned to see a shadow with a short brick physique and a glare from a pair of prescription glasses. Then a deep dark raspy voice filled the room, seemingly to vibrate the walls.

"Poisonous is the tongue of a pussy in power, your natural fear instincts blind you from the common sense that black was first and will be last. Your white purest ideology and Greco roman rule is only a cough in the millennia of history of the original man. Your lack of testicular fortitude to admit your lies and fraudulence, and despicable agenda, only speaks to your unworthiness to walk this sacared world." The mysterious wide muscular figure slowly emerged from the darkness, approaching Ron, still speaking. "Like a virus, a parasite, you came in the night and spread your cancer to everything in sight, brought death to everything you touch. But like all sicknesses, there's a cure, a natural cure....Me. And my job is to rid this Earth, our home, of the Devils that brought hell to our heaven. So, consider this a cleanse for you and those who think as you think, act as you act. You're the gunk that fills our organs, killing us slowly. A vicious gunk that overtime, has shown no regard for peace, unity, healthy living, and love. It's for that reason I will now give you a piece of the hell you tried to create, the hell you yourself fear."

"Well speak of the devil, you're right on time cuz!" Azzi turned and said in relief.

Kano smiled, "Ha! Well, shit just got extremely real for y'all," he said while looking down on the men draped in sweat, blood, and now blinding fear.

Azzi walked over and gave him a hug! "Greetings Cuz, despite the circumstances, I'm delighted to see you! Glad you could make it on such short notice! She turned to me and said. "Syr, do you remember my cousin, TY?"

That's when it hit me, Badger! I met him many years ago before he went on the run from the Government. After a nationwide search, everyone was sure he had left the country and disappeared or worse, captured by one of the many rightwing militias that wanted his head. Selah and the Badger worked close together during the Protect the People Campaign. Selah had created a private security company that hired, trained, and paid people from the community to patrol and do what cops were supposed to do, 'Protect and Serve.' At first, there were many setbacks and with 24/7 bad coverage from news stations, the people began to doubt the plan. Though within a short period of time, crime decreased drastically, it wasn't until Selah introduced TY, "The Badger" Bazgar as Top General that things really turned around. Badger is an ex-marine and world champion cage fighter, who had ties to the dark side of St. Louis. He brought ethics, order, and trust to the PPC. The people loved TY, but most importantly, they respected him. Anyone who was on some foul, stealing, and killing type crimes, had to deal with the PPC before the police got them. For shooting and any unwilling harm was forbidden. Badger and Selah created neighborhood post and safe houses, installed brighter street lights, speed bumps, and home cameras. They worked and made 40% of the churches in the city 24/7 institutions where a variety of services were offered. They teamed up to push all the liquor stores out, except for five black family-owned stores placed strategically throughout the entire city. Badger and the PPC even began signing local artist, sending some on marketing and music tours throughout the Midwest to promote the People and the new progressive St. Louis.

It wasn't until Badger realized the youths were becoming enticed with the knowledge and physical strength of the PPC and community officers. So, he and Selah decided to start teaching them. With afterschool sessions on the martial arts and combat, along with community building classes, survival, and life hacks. The work that came from the collaboration between the two changed the Lou forever, deputizing over 1500 community officers, and training over 5000 youths. Also equipping the city with the most resources the children and the state has ever seen.

Years passed with untold success of the PPC. Though the streets were becoming safer, we still had issues with violence among the youth. Badger and Selah had the great idea to create The Friday Fights. A day of competitive exhibitions in fighting and individual sports. Their influence around the city brought many people to the dynamic event, signing up community members from all over of all age ranges. After fulfilling the requirements, members allowed quarreling community members to put on the gloves to spar. They chose from a variety of now commonly learned fighting disciplines, such as Wing Chun, Krav Maga, Boxing, Brazilian Jiu Jitsu, wrestling, and many others. This worked to settle out issues, counsel, then squash all beefs. Well organized and managed, it quickly became a tradition gathering families from all over the city, bringing an end to most neighborhood rivals.

One Friday evening after the Fights, Daveon "Big Fuzz" Smith Jiles and a group of his guys were walking back to their respective hood. Big Fuzz was a known bruiser and was undefeated in the ring. Badger trained Big Fuzz himself. Allegedly on their way home from the fights, the boys were attacked by a rival hood. Four boys were shot, two died, and Big Fuzz went missing. The community was in shock and devastated. The Lou hadn't seen a crime like that in years, but nobody was hurt like Badger. Day after day, the community searched for Big Fuzz and answers on the shooting. Weeks passed before the report came out stating the shooting, murder, and kidnapping was gang related. The findings flooded the news and internet, bashing the entire PPC. The fights came to an instant halt. People were infuriated and became restless. A few days after the report surfaced, Selah received intel on the whereabouts of Big Fuzz. An old farm in Fenton. That same night, he devised a plan then headed to the location with Badger and a team of men. Armed to the teeth, they strategically raided the abandoned farm only to find Fuzz stuffed behind old machinery, shot 23 times. The team examined the body and came across three teeth implanted in the left hand. Badger and Selah collected two of the teeth and some residue they found under Fuzz's fingernails. They told the team to fall back. They then called the local police. After an investigation and results from the body, the courts said they found no evidence and had no suspects. Badger and Selah knew there was foul play. They took the teeth and residue to a close friend that worked at the hospital. Days later, they received a call with the results. The skin under the nails and teeth belonging to two different men. But they could only identify one match, Bobby McClownface, the son of State prosecutor, Jack McClownface. Those were his teeth in Fuzz's hand. They immediately took the newly-found evidence to the courts but it was all dismissed. They fought tooth and nails to get the evidence used for the case, but it was repeatedly dismissed. Another black boy murdered with justice denied right in our face. The community knew the truth but like many, many, many times before, we were shown this justice system was simply not built for us. Several months passed and things began to calm down. Then one day, on the news, it popped on the screen, "Breaking News; State attorney found slain in dumpster behind courthouse"! Names of people he put behind bars where carved on his body. But it didn't stop there. Over the next 2 months, 3 Politicians, 2 Judges, the chief of police, and 15 cops had come up either dead or missing. It took a while but eventually, they got wind of Badger's missions, unfortunately for them, they were too late. It was said he escaped to Africa and was to be hiding out in the Congo. Others heard rumors of New Zealand and India. But we were all wrong, he had never left the Lou. On the run for years, right under their noses.

"Yes, of course, we met many years ago! It's an honor to still have you with us, hate to have to be reacquainted on such a stressful occasion," I said, snapping out of my daze.

"Yea, you better! That's a Triple OG right there!" Kano said, still standing in the cut holding his drink. Standing like an old school Crip from the West coast.

"Good brother Kano, I see you haven't changed much, that's a good thing." Badger replied.

"Well, I'm always growing wiser and evolving but my humor and ferociousness toward the cause will never change. Know that." Kano said, grinning but we all knew he was serious as a heart attack.

Badger smirked very slightly then turned to Azzi and said, "Let's start moving, we don't have much time. Kano and Syr go grab the duffle bag next to my bike outside."

"Bet," Kano replied. We headed out of the room, leaving the steam room of funk. The stench was that strong.

Walking up the steps, there was an eerie silence in the darkness. Our footsteps on the old hardwood floor seemed to be the only noise in a mile radius. Slowly navigating our way through the halls, we came across a room with a dim light flickering at the end of a narrow walkway. I tapped Kano on the shoulder to get his attention, but he had already peeped what I was looking at. We headed down the long, dark hallway, approaching the dim light at the end. As we got closer, we could hear a strong fast whisper, it was strange! We got to the doorway to see The Doc dressed in Holy Garments. He was sitting with his legs crossed, one palm facing the ceiling, the other on the forehead of a motionless Selah. You could feel the energy in the room, it was powerful. It seemed like he was taking energy from the universe and delivering it into the body of Selah. Maybe he was making sure his energy, his spirit, traveled gracefully into the essence with the Gods where he belonged, only they knew. With candles lit around his body, and sage burning, Selah looked peaceful. We stood there in silence, still not believing that the King, our leader, our brother, was now forever in the essence. Kano hurried and wiped his eyes before any tear could even think about falling and walked out of the doorway.

I stood there a few more seconds, then I followed, seemingly never noticed.

We finally made it to the bike hidden by the bush in the front of the house, which is where we found the duffle bag. We tried to pick it up, but it was really awkward, we heard clinking and shuffling as if it was filled with some sort of glass and metal. We gently grabbed the bag and stumbled through the house cautiously until we got downstairs to the cellar where Badger, Zina, and Azzi awaited us.

As we softly put the bag on the ground, Badger said, "It took y'all long enough."

"Right, you know that shit was heavy and hella awkward. The real question is, how do you carry that thing on a damn bike!" Kano replied, out of breath, making a very good point.

Badger smiled, "Where there's a will, there's a way!" he said as he began to kneel down to unzip the bag. He looked back at the 3 men who were silent and exhaustedly hanging on to their lives. He looked at his watch, then looked at Azzi and said, "It's time for y'all to go! They will be looking for you soon. Find a duck off and stay out of dodge until you come up with your next move. You must disappear from here and follow the path home, they await you."

"What about the clowns that killed Selah?" Kano asked.

"They get to stay here with me. I'll find you when it's time. Now scram!" Badger said.

I grabbed my glass and took the last shot to the head then threw the glass in the furnace.

"Peace and Love cuz," I heard Azzi say as she hugged him goodbye.

Kano and I said peace and love to the OG as we headed out of the door. On our way, I stopped and looked down that long, narrow hallway where our king, Azzi's farther, was resting peacefully in the essence. The hallway was dark, the dim flickering light from the candles burned no more. Selah was with the gods and his Kingdom was left to us. Not knowing the next time I would have the chance, I said my farewells, then rushed out of the door. We jumped in the car, Kano driving, I was shotgun, Zina and Azzi were sitting in the back. The engine roared as we took off down the dark street, only to stop at the stop sign at the corner. We sat there in silence, but our thoughts could fill Madison Square Garden 10x over. So much shit happened so fast, so much shit. I mean, we just finished torturing 3 cops! Cops! The cops that murdered the leader of our movement, the father of my best friend and in a way, the father of our generation. Badger is alive, well, and ruthless as ever. You think they're not looking for those three fuck boys. AHHH! My mind is moving a million miles a minute, and who knows what's going to happen next. I'm bouncing off the walls of my skull, but in reality, I'm sitting silent, looking out of the window, staring pass the stars. A sniffle came from the backseat and broke the silence, it was Azzi. I snapped out of my daze and momentarily hushed my speeding thoughts and turned to her. She was looking down at the seat as a tear twinkled and fell from her God particle laced skin on to the upholstery still soaked with her father's blood. She gently rubbed the seat with her hand, covering it with his blood, the same blood that runs through her. I turned around and realized this feeling wasn't going anywhere fast. I looked back out of the window, hoping to find inspiration, answers, or hope, in the night sky with the stars. Looking only to find a helicopter approaching far in the distance.

"So, what's the move?" Kano asked in a calm voice, grabbing his stash of CDs to find some riding music.

I wish I had an answer, but I didn't, nor did Azzi and Zina, neither did Kano. Silence ensued.

Kano looked back at Azzi then looked at me and said, "Right." He whipped the car left, put Pac in the radio, and stepped on the gas. The engine roared through the streets as the headlights cut through the darkness like a hot knife on butter. On the run with no destination, we were heading nowhere fast. It seemed like all I could think about is how we got here, when things could be all so simple. We're a long way from simple now.

The manipulation of information,

The uses and misuses

Causes a conglomerate of power abuses

Call me clueless confused Confucius

I didnt choose this ignorance caused by your insolence

Susceptible minds raped of innocents by oppressive vigilance

Your truth holds no resemblance to a well read vet

Your bar negatively set and unfortunate criterias often met

Self hate gets A's in your class, we's the teachers pet, force feeding

doctored lies so generations pass, generations pass...

And truths well kept

But now the melting pot melts

Aloe gel on our mental welts

Cold truths ooze profusely,

Ouuu Look at that drip,

truths spill and Ouuuuu power slips

Nothing trusted from a snakes lips

'cause truths flip scripts and now we come equipped,

Shoulders too broad too clean to hold chips

Thee rebirth of a righteous nation will flow freely through our Queens

wide hips...

Righteous Nations have been built,

From our Queens empowered lips,

and wide hips...

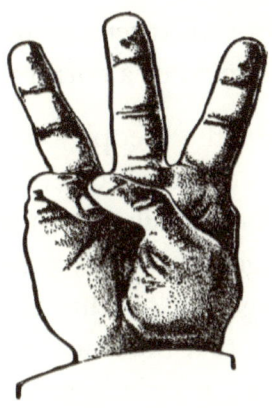

MIGHTY MIGHTY MOTHER'S UNION

Many years ago, the revolution began with the best intentions in mind. We wanted to give the people true value, power, and freedom. The very things that were snatched from many, due to the countries' destruction and manipulation of truth, image, and humanity. Politicians were being cajoled by billionaires and corporations to complete personal agendas. The government became known lap dogs to the rich. The country was so buried in debt that nations abroad began to question our economic future. We had so many private and public wars, it seemed as if we were getting paid to knock off everyone's competitors, not only our own. As it usually went, they have the goods; we have the willingness to obliterate the innocent and overthrow governments. With endless amounts of cannon fire, human and other artillery, there was no match. Black and brown countries fell, day and night due to greed and fear. The people loved and backed the soldiers like the family and fellow countrymen they were. Although many didn't believe or even know the countries' reasons for war. It seemed most were fighting just to live peacefully under the reign of a corrupt regime.

This wasn't new, but the people were starting to see the fraudulent activities from those in power more and more. Murders and scandals laced the news daily. Even the Presidents began to laugh at the laws and legislations they created. Witnessing things unfold was like watching a sick reality tv show. We didn't know what was worse, the fact that those assigned to protect and serve were killing us or our own people in power that sat and watched, refusing to cross the sticky blue line.

United in the belief that it was government over people and not people over government. All they wanted was more power and money, though the American dollar lost its value many decades ago. Unfortunately, they still had no problem doing whatever to get it. For the people, all they ever wanted was peace of mind. While they were laughing at the top, they didn't hear the people plotting at the bottom.

With the increasing population, inflation outpacing middle class salaries, and job outsources, the economy was heading down the drain. Immigration brought millions ready to work and labor for pennies on the dollar. Along with new technology, service and labor, jobs were disappearing rapidly. Online shopping itself closed 1000's of malls and stores. In numerous cities, jobs were incapable to pay the cost of living, forcing many to get multiple jobs just to survive. If you had kids, daycare alone on average was 11k a year, taking large portions of the middle and lower-class salaries. As college debt across the country increased, many graduates didn't see financial freedom until many years after being in their profession, if they were lucky to get hired. Not to mention, after a few bad oil deals, tariff disputes, and rigged elections, it was rumored that USA was going to be sold to Russia and China, if we couldn't create a stable economy. An economy that benefited all, not just those who knew the loopholes and willing to manipulate.

For decades, whites swim in freedom and privilege. Many traveled the world in war attempting to conquer other humans. Many followed their dreams of riches and adventure. Some became addicts, others lived normal working lives, but most never bore children. Now, the once majority, were only a few more years from being the new minority.

My uncle would say, "It's only because you do shit when you have money. When you're broke and hated, you stay home looking for love."

He was right, our people were broke. Studies suggested that only a few years after our numbers surpassed whites, the average household income for Blacks would be $0. Seeing as nobody was looking to spare the American African, it was time we came up with a plan to secure our own future as a people and culture or be forced to be a part of somebody else's plan, which has never worked in our favor.

Starting with just a few strong women doing small deeds around the community, and tutoring kids, something great was erected. I can remember when the Mothers' Union first formed. We were kids. At this time, kids where force-fed contemporary education about 100 years outdated. With the quickly changing economy, schools pooped out load after load of unprepared kids into a society ready to eat them alive. In most cases, that's exactly what happened. With the typical school day set up like a prison, it was easy to get lost in the system. Overcrowded classes and underpaid staff, with no resources was a sure recipe for chaos.

I can remember the madness. Kyle skipping school and getting high on the roof. Lil Zak and Dre throwing Mr. Drew stuff out the

3rd floor window while he watched. The twins going from class to class beating up dudes from rival hoods, they made it through 2 floors before walking to the office or when Tommy gave Ms. Ann the RKO in the lunchroom in front of the school. Don't even get me started on the dysfunctional parents and their traditional detrimental practices.

Bullying ran rapid and not to say, shootings in predominately white schools skyrocketed, so to think the old school system was meant for breeding social flowers was dead wrong. According to my older brother, public school in the 90's was the worse, it was said that kids were chased, beaten, or killed for having on the wrong colors, living on the wrong street, or not starting all your "C" words with "B" or vice versa. The stories are endless. It wasn't until parents woke up and realized that so much was banked on the things their child was taught in the first 17 years of their life. After thought, many parents realized they remembered very little from school. The knowledge retained served no functional purpose in the quickly evolving society.

Straight A students were working at the gas station. Which was normal for some but when Straight A students with a Bachelors and Masters began working at malls, strip clubs, and gas stations, people began to understand education inflation in a capitalistic society was real. Even some of the most loved childhood Hollywood stars were forced back into the workforce. Working side by side with the people they once called fans. Once higher education became a business, as years passed, obtaining a Masters was like having a high school diploma, only with extreme debt. Student loan debt alone was going to crash the economy. Naturally because after so long, even after paying a ton for all of that schooling, there simply weren't any jobs.

The system was set up to produce obedient workers, not thinkers and innovators. The school year was molded around multiple standardized tests. Outside of student attendance, testing meant funding for the school. Although it may not have been on purpose, it's said that TFFA hurt more students than it helped. TFFA was a teacher training and placement nonprofit with seemingly good intentions.

At that time, only 3% of the teachers were Black and less than 1% where black males. With no cultural or social experience, TFFA planted unprepared white novice teachers in at-need areas all around the nation. For a minimum of 2 years in public school, TFFA teachers could pay off student loans, causing a revolving door of teachers where stability was needed the most. Every year, student to teacher relationships were broken up. With many new rookie teachers coming in with the end in mind like a prison sentence, classroom management and fucks given, were nonexistent at least half the year. Generations of students spent 8 hours a day, 5 days a week, 10 months out of the year, for 12 straight years, learning or not learning, outdated information from socially ignorant and/or emotionally removed staff, teaching only to standardized testing. It was time for it to go!

For something so important to the mothers of the city, they knew they needed a strong leader. One willing to be the voice of reason and the hammer of purpose. That heroine was Xhosah Blu York, former state representative and Prosecuting Attorney. She was well known for her work with women and girls around the city but gained popularity when a video of her dog-walking an off-duty cop, who called her a "black nigga bitch" went viral. She then had him fired from the department. In no time, she gained the respect of the people, it was clear she was the perfect fit. With the help of Selah and the people, Xhosah Blu and the Mothers' Union spread like a wildfire! It began at one city school then spread to mothers across the state. They had a mission to bring the community together and revolutionize the educational system.

She hit the ground running! Vowing to get the community back in education, she started by teaming up with party promoters and the areas' social elite. Xhosah Blu plan was to throw the city's most extravagant workshops, retreats, parties, concerts, and festivals the state has ever seen! Raising money and earning community notoriety rapidly. The union was determined to reach their goal of getting strong, educated black mothers and fathers in the classrooms. The union used the money earned, for parent-student programs, school development, teacher incentives, community projects and much more. Providing so much support, the board had no choice but to let the union in the schools. Though at the beginning, it was tough for some of the parents, once scheduling was perfected, the old school grounds became an education community.

With parents on duty assisting around the building, behavior issues decreased. Learning sped up 10-fold, allowing teachers to explore new things in their respective field. Most importantly, community bonds were built, in and out of school.

Even with its success, there were parents that didn't like the idea of random people around their child, even though there were multiple chances to meet, interview, and build with all of the participating parents. So, though some kids left, many came with their families, prepared to be a part of the movement.

The union was created with the benefit of black children in mind, but mothers from all backgrounds and colors enlisted, and they were all invited. Their mission was to create a positive environment for kids in home and out, while giving their kids everything they needed to be prosperous anywhere, anytime equipped with truth, and knowledge. With parents now in the building, Xhosah Blu and Selah knew parents would begin to see the many falsehoods and discrepancies in the public education industry. It didn't take long. That's when Selah introduced an idea the city had never seen before. A school with innovative thought, using ancient strategies based on a curriculum created by Selah himself.

He had the great idea to combine some city schools to create a campus for youth Montessori learning and mastery. Allowing scholars K-12 to learn, counsel, and grow together in a community led institution. Though his ideas and educational beliefs were highly misunderstood, he fought diligently for the dream to come into fruition. He believed creating a Montessori University format would consistently build stronger, smarter, and more altruistic graduates year after year. This would also pool all of the funds, family, and resources from each institution into one place. Selassi University would eventually be the foundation to creating the durable affluent communities we needed across the city.

Though Selah had major blow back from city officials and residents, the majority trusted and innerstood his vision. Finally, with the help of private foreign investors and the Mothers Union, Selah began by buying and renovating the old Central Visual Performing Arts building, Beaumont, and other vacant buildings surrounding the schools along Natural Bridge Ave. Using the 132acre Fairground Park as the Intramural/Athletic fields. He then invested to bring some of the top scholars across the nation and most respected community members in the city to come teach and lead.

When finished the state of the art campus combined two high schools, Beaumont and Vashon. Two middle schools, Carr Lane and Gateway, and two elementary, Ames and Stevens. Along with hundreds of students from other schools around the city, the campus covered over 180 acres and was comprised of 12 buildings and counting. Set up like an actual university with day and night classes, and extracurricular activities. Once opened the campus seemed to never sleep.

With so much going on around campus, the implementation of peer teachers, mentors, tutors, and counseling helped to keep students ahead of the G.P.A and community service requiremnts. With the amount of wasted food and goods raising quickly in the US from 40% to 45%. As an added benefit to the community, Selah and the Union decided to provide 3 small daily meals to the students and participating parents.

By the time kids graduated they were equipped with an arsenal of knowledge and resources that could sustain them for a lifetime, even if they never learned anything else. Students knew various languages and cultures from around the world. It was required for all students to know the entire human anatomy and what's best for it, after all, it is your body. They studied masonry, agriculture and engineering. Since knowing how to grow their own food and build their own home seemed like common sense. They studied Macro and Micro economics insured their communities stayed wealthy and self-sufficient. They mastered Psychology so that human understanding was at the forefront of human interactions. That was just level 1 elementary general education studies. The innovative campus supplied vast venues to mastery to a multitude of subjects. From physical and mental sports to meta- physics, astronomy and quantum mechanics. And there was still so much more! Selassi University was the first of its kind but it wouldn't be the last.

With unheard of success, soon after Selassi University was up and running, 2 more universities modeled after it was erected around the city. The next was Mansa Tzu University which combined Sumner and Soldan, middle schools Yeatman and AAA Bush, and Bryan Hill elementary. After Mansa Tzu University came Noble Drew University. It joined Central/ROTC and Gateway High, Compton Drew, AESM, and Langston middle. The city was on a new progressive wave that was led by the ideals of Selah.

Selassi University and the others quickly rose to the top of education in the nation. Sending graduates worldwide to become some of our times greatest thinkers, leaders, and innovators. Meanwhile, most schools in the US still taught social studies filled with lies and herofication. Math that had nothing to do with economic survival, advanced thought, or worthy innovation. Science that didn't get near the tip of the iceberg of the Earths knowledge. No matter how many studies proved this to be more harmful than helpful, schools still taught around useless standardized testing. Not at The Universities, not while Selah was breathing. Selah and The Mothers Union wanted their children to think, feel, and know the best. And they were going to do it their way, taking no shorts or losses.

The community and board were astonished when the Mothers' Union proposed the idea of eradicating the chore of homework. Which the union found caused anxiety, lack of mental confidence, and didn't allow the kid to naturally fall into their own abilities and interest. No homework also allowed the kid to understand and appreciate that there is a life to live outside of school and in school. Many older community and some younger community members opposed the idea. Others took time to enroll their children in a variety of different clubs and organizations that fit their interest and skills. With the board torn, they decided to give parents the option to reject homework, if the student upheld a certain G.P.A.

Like most honor roll students, Azzi and I took full advantage. I remember after reading an ancient myth of St. Louis in *Myths, Magic, and Music Class*, Azzi vowed to change the minds of the people on the curse many believed haunted the city. The myth said that St. Louis was the Egypt of the Americas, and the Mississippi river was our Nile. In the middle, St. Louis was the heart of the country. The myth said the people of St. Louis were known for their unity and hospitality, but flourished in business, trade, and had some of the fiercest warriors across all empires. Like many empires of the early North and South America's, it thrived for 1,000's of years in unified peace, until settlers came. Being a natural people of peace, a treaty was signed, allowing settlers to trade. Little did the people of St. Louis know the settlers brought bad intentions, and even worse, their diseases. It wasn't long before disease, broken treaties, and war killed many people of St. Louis, leading to it being overtaken. As written in the myth, those that died, left their souls here to fight with the people, until the land was in the hands of the people again. With so many years of crime and violence, many community members believed the city was haunted, and criminals were possessed by the lingering Ancient spirits. Azzi wanted to change that plight. After learning of the story, Azzi began to spend her time after school reading it to younger kids. Telling the children that the souls that stayed, were warriors, Heroes and heroines, great creators and geniuses that didn't stay to haunt us, but instead, the souls stayed to motivate us to bring Royalty, Knowledge, Love, Unity and Stability back to the mighty People of St. Louis. Azzi finally told the young kids that the royal ancient souls wanted them to follow these ancient rules of the people and Earth:

1. Know & Love thy natural self; thy people and thy Mother Earth
2. Embrace community solidarity and cooperative economics
3. Develop thy spirit, mind, body, talents and character fully

4. Strive for excellence in all you do to bring honor to your ancestors and name

5. Defend the lives and the freedoms of the people

6. Don't steal, kill, or deal to thy people

7. Learn, teach then lead.

Young kids around the city learned of the myth and began to idolize the idea of having the powers, knowledge, respect, energy, and blood of such positive mythical figures. The story gave them hope and belonging.

After months of testing, the results were amazing. With kids knowing that they had to complete all work before the day was out, it naturally caused kids to do and give their best on location in the allotted time. Consequently, helping build students' confidence in all areas of education. This also allowed students like Azzi the freedom to explore, learn, teach, and serve the community in ways never thought of before. The brilliant students learned so much so fast, that it was time they reeducated, and retrained the educators.

The Mothers' Union provided top-of-the-line training with online courses, seminars, workshops and more to parents and educators. Learning together built stronger bonds and trust between the education system and the people. The school culture changed fast, the teachers that refused to evolve and remain in their traditional practices were out-shinned by newly educated parents and college volunteers. With funding from local businesses, fundraising, partnerships, tons of volunteers, and money from Xhosah's epic events; the Mothers' Union, overtime, created whatever was needed. It was done mostly by women of color, so it was hella classy. Though the Union was willing to compromise and work with the school system to create the best learning environment, they knew how to put their foot down when needed.

When met with stern opposition on key factors, the now 15k members and 500k plus social followers, let the state know their power by threatening to go on strike from work until their demands were met. Not including the numerous teachers onboard, with just the power of the mothers, banks, schools, government buildings, hospitals, the entire city would shut down. The state knew that and gave them what they wanted. With the tone set, the Union started to organize unified retreats and holidays. Collectively taking days off for mental health and other things they deemed important. Also fighting and gaining better benefits. This ultimately made for happier more productive work environments for all.

Despite criticism from officials and other districts, The Mothers' Union's first few projects were a mad success. Revolutionizing black public education in St. Louis forever. The schools where becoming powerhouses in all phases of academia, arts and athletics. Though sometimes ridiculed, the schools were becoming known nationwide, many kids wanted to attend. It wasn't long before mothers on the board joined the union. In a matter of years, innovation was spewing out of the newly joined city Universities.

During this time, although the schools where flying up the charts and crime was decreasing, our country as a whole had much more work to do. It was proven more often than we like. There were many incidents where students where followed home after class , social media threats, and crashing private events. Their salt levels were high after repeated attempts to dismantle what was built. Each year, their attempts seemed more sinister.

One year, after another dominating season for Mansa Tzu University basketball team, they met one of their biggest rivals,

Fort John Hancock High, in the state Championship game. The crowd was packed to the ceiling at the downtown stadium. Fans from both sides filled the stands. The team colors split the stadium like oil and water. Number 3 ranked Mansa Tzu University was on the road to an undefeated season and 3rd State Championship in 4 years. Fort John Hancock was having their best season in 15 years and had momentum. This game was a highly anticipated matchup that had the hopes of the city through the roof. It was time for tip off!

As the ball went into the air, so did all the eyes in the stadium. Tipped to KeRon "Kilo" Shuster, Mansa Tzu U wasted no time. Kilo, a 6'4 junior, crossed left, then right, then hit an approaching defender with a hessi, making him fall, then spinning through traffic, leaving him and Fort John's 6'10 senior star center, Tim Sharcowski. There was dead silence, you could hear a mouse fart in the packed arena. Kilo sped up and leaped off 1 foot, ball cuffed down by his waist as if he was digging in his back pocket. Tim jumped. They bumped bodies. BOOM!! Almost throwing his entire arm into the rim Kilo dunked the ball, landing on the shoulders of Sharcowski, making them both fall to the ground! The crowd erupted! Azzi hurled out of her seat in shock and aw, spilling half her FruitVeg smoothie! On the very next play, Bakari Junny King, blocked a shot that flew to half court and led to a windmill alley'oop by Eph Charles Braxthro III. The Mansa Tzu University benches almost cleared in excitement! The tone was set. At halftime, the score was 34-78 Mansa Tzu University. While the drumline and cheerleaders danced and played, contestants partook in an annual halftime Dunk Contest. The arena never stopped rocking!

With the B-team now in, ZuZu Barry, a 5'8 freshmen, kept the energy going by starting the half with a Shamgod and finger role. The JV Team didn't skip a beat.

This year, like many years in the past, the Universities had a stacked Varsity, Junior Varsity, and Freshmen team, that dominated around the country. With live streams on the Peoples University youtube channel, showing every sport, artistic, and physical/mental competition/event, the schools became ridiculously popular. They even had a channel showing the lectures from the world reowned educators and leaders. The Universities used the money from youtube for more school improvement and additions. SO the channels where always watched and the games where always packed. Selah would say, "Can't make the game...watch it on the net...no time to see it on the net, just leave it on until you go to bed." But Selah was right, the more views the channel had the more money the Universities received for expansion. Which consequently had most home games looking like concerts between every break and during halftime. The bands kept it crunk for the culture.

Azzi had the student section swag surfing the whole 3rd period. It was clear the game was over. It wasn't until 4th quarter when many of the parents and fans of Fort John Hancock High began to become angry. Taunting players and throwing trash on the court. Calling white refs, traitors and negro lovers. They even called some players circus apes because they thought the team was showing off. Soon, it was no longer about the game, with parents from both sides going at it, the game ended almost unnoticed. The bad energy overflowed outside when suddenly, a Mansa Tzu University player was hit in the head with a beer can thrown from the rival section. Azzi and I was in the middle. In a matter of seconds, a brawl was unleashed.

It got out of control so quickly, the lot turned into a mosh pit. Black, Brown, and pink people were throwing punches everywhere all willie nillie! Confused in the midst of the chaos, I turned to look for Azzi. She was gone!

Ducking, bobbing, weaving, pushing my way through, I yelled her name and searched for her. "Azzi! Azzi!"

There was no answer, if she could even hear me over the mayhem. Turning and looking frantically, I suddenly hear "Bitch!" I turn around to see Azzi in mid-air, kicking a rival's chunky soccer mom in the chest. The lady fell, tearing a hole in her jorts. She rocked and rolled until she made it to her feet then retreated into the crowd. I began to run and push my way through the crowd until I got to her.

"Come on! Let's go!" I yelled, trying to grab her.

She snatched away from me and said, "Nah! These hoes got us messed up! Don't worry about me! Protect your people!"

I turned to see a man with a flush red face running my way with his fist balled to attack. I immediately pushed Azzi out of the way. I then instinctively slipped his odd and loosely thrown punch. The infuriated attacker, red with anger, stumbled off balance, then tripped awkwardly and slowly, until he planted his face against a parked car. Knocking himself unconscious. Then out of nowhere, we heard gunfire from across the lot.

The crowd rushed the streets in fright, looking for shelter and a way out. Azzi and I ran for cover behind a truck parked across the street. Then ran along the parked cars down the street until we were clear of trouble.

"You see that shit?!" I said, still jogging to keep up with Azzi and the crowd.

"Man, I hope nobody died!" Azzi replied, looking back.

"I'm sure we're going to hear all about it at school or on the news! The bus to the west comes in 3 minutes. Let's catch that bih!" I said, looking at my watch. We ran and made the bus just in time.

It wasn't long after making it to Azzi's home we found out someone from Hancock was shot but was in stable condition at the hospital. Shortly after watching the story on the shooting victim, a breaking news alert went across the screen. When the video hit the screen, our mouths dropped to the floor in disbelief. Mansa Tzu University was up in flames. Burning slowly to the ground and into the past. So many emotions of fury, hate, regret, sadness, went through our bodies, we didn't know where to begin. We would have to begin somewhere in order to heal.

After the school tragedy, when things calmed down, the district split Mansa Tzu University with Selahassi and Noble Drew University until the school was built back to its original luster. It was awkward at first, but we were always welcoming. Azzi and I introduced ourselves to everyone on the first day of the joining. That's where we first met Zina.

Yung Bulls Yung Bulls,

come together, remove that wool,

Blind with no direction so you push and pull!

Remove that wool!

You're no fool

You're no tool

The trap is cool, that's the trick,

its shiny fun and full of chicks, sheeps, pigs, & wolves in wigs,

that are holistically sick & dearly derelict,

what a lick,

Blood suckin ticks watch you tick tick boom,

condemned to doom fresh out the womb,

because of Illest diets you consume

The cycle recycles

But to whom?

Use your focus to zoom and catch the scent,

use that tool between your ears to become extra competent,

extra resilient, super intelligent,

build and build on your benevolent worldly cultural relevance…

Whoa whoa Yung Bulls Yung Bulls

you're reaching heights,

bright new heights,

youre taking flight,

servant leaders showing might,

erasing fading plights…

Whoa whoa Yung Bulls Yung Bulls

stay together,

Hold on tight, Be the light,

be the fight for right

Be the light,

be the fight for right,

when its bright & even in the night,

hold on tight

In The darkness be the light,

Not inspite,

be the fight for right,

until right is all that is in your sight

Until you change your plight and right is all that is in our sight.

Easy easy Yung Bulls Yung Bulls all will be alright

The sun is out and the harvest is here, take a bite of what we made ripe

All will be alright...

THE COMMUNITY CURE FAIR

zzi and I were sitting alone in the lunch room, watching the breaking news of another school shooting, this time in Florida. It was the 20th of the year and it was only February. The world watched as news anchors and representatives spewed words of understanding and concern, claiming mental issues, disturbed upbringing, and guns. Though crime was drastically decreasing in our city, around the country terrorist activity from Euro-Americans was on the incline. Despite what the media said, "whites" held down the top spots in the categories of mass killings and rapes since the first boat hit the shore. A fact many went to great lengths to deny.

Having had enough, Azzi stood and unplugged the TV. "Right." she said sarcastically in a low tone.

That's when we heard a voice from the back of the cafeteria. "Gracias, no podria tomar otro Segundo de narracion blanca sobre el salvajismo blanco!- Thank you, I could not take another second of white narrative about white savagery!"

We turned around and saw a broad-shouldered woman with a fro, she was using tools bending copper wiring, while guarding a cup of tea.

Azzi and I walked over, noticing this was a student we haven't met before. Approaching her table, strong posture, she stood and said, "Please check your energies before entering my realm family."

Azzi and I looked at each other oddly.

Azzi replied, "Energy checked, good vibes only around here! We just wanted to introduce ourselves and check out this magical ass fro you rockin sis! I'm Azzi. What's your name?!"

"Hahaha! Magical? Tah, girl thanks but you know how much work I got to put in just to be able to leave the house! These fingers, my juices and berries are magical fug you mean?!" she said, sharing a good laugh with Azzi! "I'm Zina by the way, who's that?"

I stood there, awkwardly staring at her copper creations.

"Oh, that's just Syr weird ass, he cool though," Azzi volunteered. Everyone laughed.

"Damn, you already hatin' and we just met! It's nice to meet you sis, don't listen to her ass, she's the crazy one. But low key, you probably crazy as hell too while you talking!" I said.

"We all have a little crazy in us!" Zina replied.

We all laughed and laughed hysterically! "What are you back here making anyway, it looks dope?" Azzi then asked.

Zina grinned and said, "Oh y'all gone love this!" She made a few more alterations then held up 2 shinning swirl copper bracelets. She then slid both on and reached into her bag and said, "This gone kill 'em right here though y'all." She pulled out a gleaming copper crown covered in purple rubies.

"Daaaaamn!" Azzi said in amazement!

It was gorgeous and truly fit for a queen. She lifted the crown and placed it upon her rich curly melanated mane. She stood and lifted her chin, we looked in awe as she posed, resembling an amazon Goddess or Queen of many nations.

"Ouuu!! I want one! Do you sell them!" Azzi asked.

"Of course, girl you look like you should already have one on!" Zina replied.

"I know right! I'm glad you know because people be acting like they ain't hip!" Azzi proclaimed.

"Aye, don't be making her head any bigger than it already is, her bonnets already look like fitted mattress sheets," I said, chiming in. We burst into laughter!

"Yo mama bonnets look like fitted sheets, you asshole!" Azzi replied, laughing.

That's when the bell rang! Ever since that day, we've been partners in crime.

Zina fit right in with us, an intellectual that loves her people and having fun. Our friendship instantly began to grow. Like most years prior, since the Mothers' Union, the revised school district held its annual Community Cure Science Fair! Which was like a science fair of old, but on steroids. Azzi and I skipped the fair last year, we were tired from our community compose and energy project. Which led to us collecting tons of trash and old half eaten food. The winner received sponsorship and donations to fund their projects. Some helped others scratch the surface but most rarely assisted the community in any major way for long periods of time. We didn't see how this year was going to be different. But it was, there was prize money!

One day after school, Azzi, Zina and I, headed to Shareef's for a study session we called Books, Baking, Building, and Blunts. It was something a group of us did after school every once in a while. We discussed books, baked snacks, brainstormed on community solutions, and of course, chiefed untampered strains of the stickiest of the icky. We were looking to get some ideas and inspiration for this year's Science Fair. Shareef's was the "station for creative motivation" so he called it. Shareef was one of the smartest people I knew, his library was stacked, he taught himself to do and know so many random things. Shareef dropped out of school 2 years before to pursue a private family business in Herb pharmaceutics. Which was a booming industry. He left with straight A's. Reef always said that school just wasn't for him. As the former captain of the football team, everyone was surprised when he left school. I could tell in class; his thoughts were far away from school, possibly far away from everybody else's thoughts.

I remember in Advance History class, he and the teacher got into a heated debate. While discussing one of the many white atrocities in history hidden from us, Shareef uttered under his breath, "Bruh, what's the point of this shit?"

Mr. Wise turned around, "What was that young brother?!"

"Nothing," Shareef replied.

Mr. Wise stopped class to address, "No, please enlighten us Shareef, class listen up, the Football captain has something to say."

Everyone turned and looked at Shareef sitting deep in the back of the class. "Speak your mind brother!" Mr. Wise suggested.

Looking around at all of the eyes on him, Shareef said, "I said ain't no point in spending all this time learning old shit!"

The class gasped, Mr. Wise calmed everyone and said, "It's ok, let's discuss, what makes you say that young brother?"

"Man, I'm not trying to be disrespectful, but every day we come in here, we're learning about some old, horrible thing these Mayonnaise monkeys did to us! Just about everyday, how is that helping us progress? I don't see the point OG," Shareef said with conviction.

"If we're going to have this discussion like adults, before we move on, promise that'll be the last disrespectful comment you make about anybody of any color or background," Mr. Wise said.

"My bad," Shareef replied.

Mr. Wise walked to the front of the class. "I will tell you why I believe it is a dire need for our youths to know the past. It's because for many years, the truth was hidden from us, so much was lost, and for many years, our people believed lies of being savages from a dark land. Lies of being slaves and so much more. They erased our leaders, role models, and culture we took thousands of years to create. Math, science, better ways of life, and more. Hidden or erased. Without that, many had no hope of a better day. So, we teach the past to ensure that our future generations know we're Kings, Queens, and even Deities. But also teach it to ensure we as a people don't make the same mistakes again."

The class applauded in praise of Mr. Wise's response. Shareef clapped as well then said, "Mr. Wise, I feel that 100 percent. I just feel like when moving forward, only a fool would trip over things that's behind him. While we're learning stuff that's a 1,000 years old, they're learning things that's 100 years into the future. Staying many steps ahead of us, while we're steady going backwards. They're tapping into new forms of energy, building weapons, and traveling space while just a few years ago, the biggest thing on our mind was the race/color of a folklore. There are 1,000's of guys that fought the good fight and died. Their followers scattered like roaches with their beliefs tucked between their legs. Showing us everyday that despite all the good shit those good brothers did, and all the good stuff you're teaching, anyone of us can be stopped and killed for nothing. Over some mess people only half-ass believe in anyway. I mean, I get it but I also believe it's stuff like this that stunt the growth of our people. We got a knife in our back, they've pulled it out a little, and we're praising that, as if the knife still in our back isn't killing us anymore. It's too much money and future, Mr. Wise. I'm tired of hearing what a king used to be like, tell us how to be a king in present day society. This old stuff ain't making negroes no money, you been in the game for 20 plus years and you stay in an apartment on the Northside and drive a 2001 Buick. From the outside looking in, knowing this stuff hasn't been very good to you fam. But you fight that good fight OG while I secure this bag."

The class was silent, stumped and enlightened at the same time. Mr. Wise took a deep sigh and said, "Son, I really hope you figure this life out, it's more than you think. It's especially more than a bag of money."

"Yea, me too," Shareef said, closing his textbook. Then the bell rang. That was the last time he was ever in that class.

On our way to Shareef's home in Baden for the "Study", Zina Azzi and I discussed possible projects, innovative ideas, and books to discuss once we got there. "Aye, y'all know how people say dogs can smell different types of cancers!? What about dog sniff detectors? They sniff people to see if they can smell a disease! They'll save hella lives," Zina said out of nowhere.

"Girl what? Who the hell 'bout to walk thru and let random ass dogs sniff all in they booty to look for coodies!" Azzi said, laughing and sniffing Zina like a crazy dog.

"It look like you go around sniffing ass," Zina said with a straight face. Which made me burst into laughter.

"It do though," I said, chuckling.

They both turned to me with a blank stare. "Shut yo uglass up, we know for a fact you done sniffed some booty, don't make us ask Neffy!" Azzi said, starting to laugh.

"Sike! She cool, but never am I sniffing no cakes!" I proclaimed. Even though Neffy was very sniff-worthy.

"Yea OK!" Zina added.

The Bus was approaching our stop in Baden. "But forreal though, what about service buses for hygiene, food, gas, water, or whatever the community votes for or something? Maybe even slap some solar panels and rims on that bih! They can roll through all day on a schedule. Like regular buses," I asked as the bus stopped and we jumped off.

"That's actually not a bad idea, but can we talk about it once I get some of this food in my stomach. I'm starting to not feel like myself, like I want to curse somebody out for no reason," Azzi said as we headed down the street towards the house.

"Girl you know, it ain't nothing but pastries this time," I said.

"Boy, I don't care. I'm hungry as fuck, and you 'bout to make me curse you out," Azzi said, speeding up and walking ahead.

"Let me text this dude to open the door, before her special self go knocking like she the boys," I mumbled to myself.

"Yea, do that," Zina added, giggling.

Finally, at Shareef's home, as we approached the porch, the door swung open. There stood Shareef in an apron with no shirt on, covered in tattoos.

"Faam Laaay! Young Gul what's good my nig!" Shareef yelled from the porch.

"Reef! What's the word family!" I replied in excitement, happy to see the good friend!

"Sup SiStas! Welcome to Mi Casa. I already got some goods in the oven! Come on in!" Reef said, greeting the ladies as they walked in.

When I walked in, there were books everywhere! Random graffiti signatures all over the walls and a salad bowl full of bud! Though this wasn't my first time to his place, I always marveled at the book collection he obtained. He had a section that covered all world religions, scriptures, economy mastery, finance, music, history and culture. We took off our shoes and headed to lounge where the sessions were held.

"What's been up bro, how's the matrix treating you and the posse?!" Reef said, laughing.

"Matrix?! You crazy, what I tell you about being under a rock for too long, Selah and the Union been making strides!" I replied.

"Strides towards what though? The countries new version of Liberty? Y'all gone get enough of living within the parameters of this perceived oppressor. The growth is being dictated by the leanisy of primitive minds with power. And y'all give them power by asking instead of just turning y'all back and making unified moves. That's how you get true freedom, not liberty. Y'all negroes love some liberty with a splash of false direction. Low key, everything could stay the same at the core, but if y'all had more materials and nonsense, many of y'all wouldn't even care about what's really going on," Shareef said, laughing and setting a stack of books on the table.

"And here he go. Y'all didn't waste any time, huh?" Azzi said, pulling her books out of her backpack.

"Hol'up, what you mean y'all? Never am I loving any form of this mess! That's you Nemrod!" Zina said, seemingly getting agitated.

"I smell pastries, come on, let's go see what he has!" Azzi said, changing the subject and grabbing Zina. They got up and went into the kitchen.

Shareef grabbed a handful of bud out of the bowl and a wrap. "What I meant by matrix is way of life. People consume themselves in the matrix without even knowing. Knowing nothing outside of what you see on tv, or on Bookface. Generational matrix! Negroes start off hearing false ideologies of power and social placement early on from parents who ain't never did nothing outside of working, fuckin, drugs, and going to church. It's a reason people act like this and believe what they believe. Acting like their surroundings don't affect their behavior. Or people don't spend trillions of dollars just to make sure you watch certain shit at certain times. Or how hard it was for Xhosah Blu York to change out them books, just for 3 schools bro. It's a war going on for your brain and people not even hip," he said, breaking down the bud and rolling up. Now licking it closed.

"Yea bro, fuck them, the people should just turn their back and do them low key," he continued.

I sat there, listening to his words as I joined him in the sessions traditional rolling ceremony. "High Key, what you mean! It's fools out here that love the bliss their ignorance brings, shit, it's so bad now that people would die and kill to stay stupid. But what I can say, is that, more people are waking up and seeing the shit show that's going live right in their faces," I replied.

"Right. Unfortunately, most are just entertained by it because their lives are shit shows as well," Reef added, laughing and padding himself looking for his lighter.

That's when Azzi and Zina came back from the kitchen with 2 platters of pastries, and some natural fruit drinks. "Ohh, I'm so hungry I can't wait! So what books do y'all have today?" Azzi said, putting the tray on the table.

"*I got The Life Sciences of Living Off Grid in The City*, and umm, *The Secret Mind and Math of The Melanated*," Reef said.

"Umm I have, *Common Ethics and Morals for Universal Human Progression*," I answered. "What y'all got, while you asking us?" I continued.

"I only brought, *They Came Before Columbus: The African Presence in Ancient America* by Ivan Van Sertima." "And I have the same from last time we conjugated," Azzi and Zina replied while stuffing their face with food.

"Doesn't look like it matters but they're vegan pastries by the way," Reef said with a look of amazement of how hungry the girls where.

We joined them in having a vegan pastry. It was delicious! "What the hell you put in this? Crack!? It's nutritious and delicious, family!" I said with a full mouth.

"Ain't it though!" Azzi added. I ate another.

After enjoying my last pastry, I cleaned my hands and said, "Let's focus on this project, let's see if we can get that lil bread they're giving away!"

"Yeah, let's do that. Weren't you talking about some buses or something? I'm sorry I wasn't listening, I was hungry," Azzi said with a smile and taking another bite.

"Before we build any further, let us fire up the blunt and indulge in the stickiest of the ickiest! Join me, family!" Reef said, setting a blaze to the stogie filled with herb.

As the flame went around the room, we discussed different solutions to community problems or ways to improve the advancements we have already had. Vibing to the tunes of Goodie Mobb and Currency, along with some other great southern artist. But mostly, local underground music, we loved that raw sound.

With the air spiked with clouds of herbal spirit, it came to me; "TV lenses that increase picture quality, you can buy them from the store and their made out of recycled tv screens," I said, checking the stock market.

"Bro, we tryna get fools to stop watching Tv, not see the bs better," Reef said, chuckling and flipping through the pages of his book.

"Man, that'll revolutionize TV! You tripping," I said with confidence.

"Eh, my hearts not in it, sorry boo!" Azzi said, taking another bite of her pastry.

"Next! Nah I'm playing, but what about fruit trees and gardens planted throughout the streets, we could feed the community forever," Zina said, typing on her laptop, researching.

"Man, people hella sketchy, how you know some random creep not gone come treat the trees with poison or something. Have everybody sick?" Reef said, still reading.

"What if it was just at lil tree parks at different places around the community? We can have community guard times. And since it's free, we could only let them pick from the trees at private events. Then just put the pickings out at the stand for the public. Keeps everything somewhat safer. The money raised at the private events can go to building more parks around the city," Zina added.

"I can see them parties being hella classy but lit though, as long as it ain't no angry squirrels or bats in those trees or something," Azzi volunteered, praising the idea.

"I Like that too, family. I get to sport my apple green forces," Reef said, hitting the L.

"Actually, I was thinking we should make people wear slippers when picking. Soooo, you can keep them uglass shoes at home if you like," Zina said sarcastically.

Azzi and I burst into laughter as Reef just grinned and wiped off his shoes.

"Ok write that one down with the rest of the good ones. Let's keep going!" I said, taking a drink of my freshly squeezed dark berry, wheat grass, banana, and pineapple nectar. It was exquisite the way Zina made this drink, it was a glimpse of her mastery. Either that or I was fried.

"Solar panel car electric kits for old gas cars!" Reef said with confidence.

"Who finna make that mess? You?" Azzi said.

"Yea, as Azzi said, my heart's not in it Reef," Zina added.

"Damn, y'all shoot stuff down faster than scary cops with daddy issues," Reef said, chuckling.

"Boy you know it's all love we got to keep it 100 and keep it moving! I would want you to do no less with me," Zina said.

"Let's try energy generating exercise equipment in schools and gyms," Reef added. "Now that's a good one team!" I said, writing the idea on the growing list.

"What about roof windmills to help communities make their own energy?" Azzi suggested. She received a thumbs up from the team and her idea made the cut.

I came up with solar panels made from recycled CD's and old electronics, but the idea was shot down when Zina said, "Man, don't nobody listen to no CD's nomore dude!"

Reef later came up with manmade Water Holes and fountains. The idea was to end the mass production of single use items, which was a great idea to me, but it got even better when Azzi added on personal utensils, reusable trays, plates that could be bought in stores and restaurants.

It wasn't until Reef added, "Let's make edible dishes as well that we can sell to stores and restaurants." That's when it became epic. It was another one on the list.

Though we had a list full of great ideas, we wanted to keep going until one touched us all. After some more guesses, Zina suggested bio waste energy. It had to do with turning food scraps and human waste into energy and fertilizer at home with a reusable waste water supply. Which was kind of like the project we did the year before.

We were starting to slow down and the ideas where getting worse and worse and nobody was in love with any of the ones we had already. Reef fired up again and the blaze went in orbit around the stacked centerpiece of books. As I felt elevated and lifted to an ease of mind allowing my mind to wonder aimlessly. Man, the power of herb, no wonder every dang artist in the past stayed high. I thought to myself as I was gazing into the universe behind my eyelids. Then like a brick, it hit me.

I leaned up and took another drink, then I blurted out, "What about Hemp?" There was a few seconds of silence.

Then Zina chimed in and said, "Weed negro? What about some hemp are you speaking of?"

"Shid hemp everything really. It can be used to make so much," I added.

"But how is it helping the community for this project, bro?" said Reef.

"I mean, we can have the community take over the industry. We can start a hemp clothing line with eco-friendly materials. Have the people grow it. It can be bigger than cotton, you can do 10x more stuff with it," I explained.

"Eh, I don't know, banking on commitment from large amounts of people to do extraneous work is sketchy. We'll end up doing most of it ourselves," Azzi added.

"What if we just start it off as a dropshipping company from a hemp clothing manufacture? Start a campaign, sell and stack until we have enough to make it bigger. Low upfront cost too and no merchandise to worry about. Plus, we got some models right here!" Reef said, grinning at the ladies.

"We can make that happen. Sounds easy as well. This can be big!" Zina proclaimed.

"Is it better than the other ideas tho?" Azzi asked.

"Nah, but it seems more practical and less stressful. Especially if we find a way to get the community involved. Worst case scenario is that we will have a lit ass clothing line," I said as the smoke that flowed through the room threaded between our vessels. Silence ensued. We sat, vibing to the tunes, soaking in the thoughts and possibilities of this epic idea.

After a few minutes passed and few more orbits of the blaze. "So, it seems like this is the one. What are the next steps, family?" Azzi said, breaking the silence.

We listed some steps and created and execution timeline.

It was starting to get late and it was already past my time to be home. Zina had no curfew and Azzi had to get home before Selah. So Azzi, Zina and I packed up our stuff, said farewell to Reef and headed back to the Westside with a plan that could change the landscape of the entire city.

On the way back on the bus, we saw the many faces of our people leaving the corporate plantation. Drained, beat, and unmotivated about the future. It was like this every time we rode the bus, filled with people that are just living to work and working to live. I feared that plague of unhappiness and contentment most people suffered from. The thought of living your entire life, doing something I don't want to do, muting your urges for more because you know you will have to sacrifice more than you can lose. I demised the notion of that existence for myself, even though so many around me indulged in that way of life. For me, it all began at home.

We were approaching their stop. I always walked them to Azzi's home when we got off the bus, then walked the rest of the way to my crib. As we came up to her large Westside city home, you could hear the barks of the infamous dogs. They were puppies but already big enough to jump the gate. They were known to chase outsiders to the edge of the block then come back into the yard.

Walking up the steps to the door, I saw the curtain peep open then a deep voice said, "Easy," silencing the dogs, the door unlocked and swung open. Revealing his large frame, there he stood. "Lil girl, y'all cutting it close. Syr, you're supposed to make sure they're here since they're with you! Come on in here," Selah said, letting us in and closing the door.

Selah was almost never there, always moving around with different projects around the city with his team. He always used to say he was busy making the bed for his grand babies. Selah, the man that helped build the school I attend, he's why there's a man on every corner making sure kids are safe. He's the founding father of so many of the positive changes our community has seen in the last 50 years. Even after accomplishing so much, he was still humble, down to earth, and a real St. Louis OG.

"So, lil big head babies, tell me how y'all day went," he said, hugging and giving Azzi a kiss on the head.

"It went well! We're entering into the Community Cure Science Fair. How was yours?!" Azzi replied.

"Yea, we're about to get that bag Unc," Zina added, putting her stuff down and flopping down on the couch.

"We making clothes out of weed Pops, all Syr's idea too," Azzi said, grabbing something to drink out of the refrigerator.

Everyone turned and looked at me. I looked around then grinned and said, "Do y'all blame me though?" Everyone burst into laughter!

"Let me find out y'all smoking some damn weed! Y'all two ain't mine but I'll beat you like you are!" Selah said.

"Whoa, that went left fast, we're joking family, no need to beat nobody down big fella!" I said, laughing to ease whatever mild tension that may have existed.

"It's hemp, not actual weed Pops. We're going to show everyone the benefits and many uses of this crop. We only got the resources for the clothes now though," Azzi said.

"Oh word! That's dope, what all can you do with it?" Selah asked, sitting down and grabbing his gallon of fruit and veggie water.

"Umm. Bricks, different oils, you can make whatever you want out of it really, it's easy to grow, clean, efficient, and it's good for your body," I answered, trying to remember my notes.

"Better than clay and metal though?" Selah asked.

"In a way. I mean, you don't have to dig in the earth to get it and you can just grow it just about anywhere. May not be totally better in some aspects, but it can replace so many things. Things that are outdated and harming the environment," Zina replied.

"Damn, imagine if someone could control that industry. Better yet some people," Selah said, rocking in his chair with a serious thinking face.

"Same thing I said," I volunteered.

"That's some genius stuff young brother, I really can't wait to see where you guys take it," Selah said, leaning on the edge of his chair in interest.

"Yea, the possibilities are endless it seems," Azzi said, now munching on a leftover sandwich.

"Right, well, family I got to get home before y'all have another roommate", I uttered.

"Aye, you always welcome here!" Azzi said.

"Says the joker that don't pay any damn bills and still colors outsides the lines," Selah hurried and replied.

Azzi rolled her eyes.

"It's all good, it looks like everyone has IBS in this house anyway," I said jokingly to ease the tension of the truth that I had to still leave and go somewhere I despised. Everyone laughed hysterically as I slowly made my exit.

"Ight Family! One love," I said as I opened the door.

"Peace out Syr!" The ladies said as I walked out of the door.

Selah walked to the door to lock it, but then walked outside with me and said. "Aye Syr, I know it's rough. But as a man, you'll have to make peace with your struggle and your past. The sooner you make peace with it, the faster you can overcome them. You just have to trust your process. You know we're here for you. Don't let the pride monster eat you alive young man. Remember life has its own beat and every young man has a verse to rap, just make sure your 16 bars are the best true representation of you. Head up and shoulders back. Meet your troubles squarely, face to face. Into the fire you go." I'll Never forget those words.

I just nodded my head, smiling. Not showing him how much I needed to hear that. "I appreciate that Selah, One love," I said then began to walk down the long, dimly lit street.

"Text Azzi when you make it home!" he yelled from the porch. I raised my hand in acknowledgment and continued to walk. I was only 3 short bus stops away from my home, so I always decided to walk, even in odd weather.

Hitting the corner to my block, I could see my people's truck parked outside. That guaranteed, I was going to have to answer for being late. This wouldn't be the first time, nor the last. I approached my house, almost eager to walk in and get everything over with. I pulled out my keys and opened the door. I walked in the house and there he was with his back to me, rocking in his chair laughing at a rerun of "Cheers".

"What's up!" I said low, hoping he didn't hear me over the noisy Tv.

"Huh! What! Syr, speak up!" he said turning and then muting the Tv.

"I just said what's up. That's all," I said, leaning to walk away.

"Did I tell you to go anywhere?" he said in a sharp but low tone. I stopped in my tracks and put my hands in my pockets. "Why are you late?" he asked.

"I was with Azzi and Zina working on a project at the library," I replied.

"A project, huh? Who is Zina, another lil knuckle head girl too dumb to stay away from yo dumbass?" he said with a slight grin on his face.

"Nah, she a new girl. She came when they combined the schools," I said.

"Right whatever, I don't have time to believe your lies. You want to be a hoe dummy. Then go ahead but get your own house first. Go be like your daddy and yo momma! Matter of fact, go live with them and do what you want to do," he said, staring into my eyes. "You hear me talking to you, look at me! You got something you want to do to me? You got something to say!?" he continued.

"Nah," I replied.

"Nah what?! Take that stupid look off your face before I slap it off!" he screamed.

"Nah, I have nothing to say," I said in a low tone.

"Get the fuck out of my face!" he said, turning the Tv off mute.

I was relieved and walked away quickly. Only to go a few feet away, to my bed in the living room of a 7-bedroom 3 story house. He used to say, he wanted us as close to the door as possible. As a constant reminder that he didn't want us there. Not allowed to get on the phone, watch tv, or go outside on weekdays, I had the hells luxury of hearing my friends play outside as I sat in isolation, for many years of my youth.

Being the youngest of 5 boys raised in a time when crack, gangs, pimps, and police shootings where at an all-time high. Dysfunction was a norm. Staying with my father in my early years didn't last long. When I was 4, he was locked up for murder. Once he was gone, our mother became an addict, and was deemed not fit to care for us. We bounced around in the system for years it seemed. From one foster home to the next. No one wanted to take the burden of 5 boys, but also nobody wanted to split us up. I'm 6 years younger than my closest brother and my oldest is 10 years my senior. We stuck together throughout the entire process. We were all we had. Until the day he came to pick us up. Excited to be leaving the packed, urine-laced foster home deep in the city, we were hopeful of a new beginning.

It didn't take long before a rift formed between my oldest brother, Kano, and him. Though young, Kano was already thoroughly engrained in a lifestyle looked down upon by our new overseer. Only a few days after a heated argument over a wad of money found in Kano s possession, my brother, Kano, was kicked out. Without any support, he instantly became a homeless teen. Not long after, he was sentenced to 10 years fed time after being caught with drugs and a gun. With the slightest clue of our life before he labeled us a burden, and that's exactly what he treated us as. The tone was set and would only go downhill from there. Serving up strict rules and unjust punishments daily just to assert his power over growing boys. Only a year had passed before my next brother ran away. The day after he graduated from high school, Charles went to the Navy. He said he would rather go to war than spend another day under that roof. Always being athletic, Earl took his first scholarship offer to play basketball at a Juco in Coahoma, Mississippi. I was all alone now. With him. We had no social relationship, we only spoke to say "hey", "Goodbye", or when I did something wrong. Without those words, I would've lived in complete silence and solitude for 98% of my stay with him. Now much older, it didn't take long before I became a social recluse.

Now secluded in my room, I put my headphones in and wondered about the details and ideas for the project. With the sound of DMX blasting in my headphones, I drifted away into thought, then into slumber.

SO much salt built up for this cult

a cycle of assault plagues the boy to man thoughts,

What you thought,

*the love drought and iron fist builds mist of self-hate around young boys'
confidence.*

*Afraid of my limitlessness, wish my fears where yours, you teach me how
to love but not how to show.*

Show me how to hurt but not grow.

Black Blossum You grow in Snow Slow

*Hidden is your glow due to shade of broken Men with pride dripping
from their chins on to your reality.*

Vomit your insecurities and shit your failures to dull a shine.

*Wish time would rewind to give you the mind to know that mine is
exceptional, brilliant, bright, fine, and my shine can blind the divine, in
due time, in due time.*

Boom Boom! Boom! I jumped out of my accidental slumber to
see him standing over me. "Wake up and go to bed and cut that
trash off!" he said, snatching the headphones off my ears.

Leaving, he hit the light and began walking upstairs. Still sitting in the same spot with my clothes on, now in the dark, I just jumped in bed and dreamt of a speedy morning sun. For me, that meant another chance to see Azzi, my breath of fresh air in a cloud of misery and false perceptions of manhood. The darkness behind my eyelids comfort me, luring me into a deep sleep.

Sunny summer evenings on the Westside of the Lou.

Jump ropes and flips, parades of happy kids enthusiastically enjoying their youth.

Smooth streets filled with bikes & the beats of the people's feet.

Young and old smiles laced with pearly white teeth.

Sheesh look at that shine, original skin covered in earth's oils, ageless making your melanin so fine.

Spit truth stronger that moonshine just to chase it with love purer than water from a jungle vine.

Prosperity cloaks the community vibes, stability across industry that can withstand the changing tides.

My people draped with pride with all the mf bs aside.

Farms of colorful goodness riddle the yards, trees of juicy fruits the size of cars that stretch for far.

Look how far, we black as tar, have come!

Bedazzled solar panels and gleaming spinning windmills that help our community run.

Daughter, wife, mother, grams stroll carefreely under the life-giving sun.

Dreams of peace and prosperity, innovation with cultural clarity were no longer a rarity.

Look how far we've come. Look how far we have come.

Ding Ding Ding! Ding Ding Ding! Ding Ding Ding!...

I was suddenly jerked out of my sleep by my screaming morning alarm.

Ding Ding Ding! Ding Ding Ding! Ding Ding Ding! It rang again as I hurried out of bed to silence the noise. Now with the alarm off, it was time for school and another chance to feel wanted, accepted, by the people I cherished most, my friends.

RITTER LIGHTENING THIEF

When I made it to school, Azzi and Zina were sitting in our usual spot in the cafeteria. "Family, Family, Family!" Azzi said across the lunchroom, stealing my signature greeting.

"Fam laaaaay!" I replied, stopping and holding my arms open.

"Hola! Please tell me you have something written down for the project," Zina said, still writing down ideas on the upcoming project.

"When have I ever let you down?" I said, digging through my messy bag, looking for the messy notes I took when I was half asleep last night. "Got it, I think y'all will like what I've come up with!" I said borderline excited.

"Gone and spill the beans please! The bell 'bout to ring!" Zina said. Flipping through the pages, I said, "What if for the project, we just show all the dope things hemp can do for an individual and the community! For the shirts, we can start a 5-year campaign where all the proceeds from sold merchandise can go to rebuilding hoods around the city. The idea is to get a mass amount of people to buy gear from us for 5 years straight. The fashion industry funnels billions of dollars annually, we only need a piece of that to make a difference. We may not be able to get much of a bag now but if niggas buy into the idea, think of all the bread we'll raise for needed community projects!"

"So, getting everybody in the Lou to invest in one brand to help rebuild the community? Wow, he does have a brain, Zina," Azzi said, grinning at me.

"Indeed, he does!" Zina added.

"Right, I got more than that, wink wink!" I said, laughing and blushing.

"Just had to sprinkle some lame on the joke huh. Good job," Zina said, taking my notebook and looking through my notes. "But low key, I think this can work y'all! What is People Power Prosperity?" she continued.

"That's the name I thought of! Get the People, Gain the Power, bask in Prosperity," I replied.

"Damn, that's deep, I love it!" Zina said, knocking some dust off my shoulders.

"Well, ain't nothing to it, but to do it!" Azzi said with jolly enthusiasm.

Zina and I looked at her with blank expressions. "Now that was lame," I said, taking my notebook back from Zina.

"Anyway, how about Azzi set up the website, Zina you research hemp product distributors, and I can come up with some designs and marketing schemes. What y'all think?" I added.

"Yea, I can do that, what about you, girl?" Zina said to Azzi.

"Yea, I already have a dope format in mind!"

Ring, Ring, Ring, Ring!

"Damn, that bell is annoying!" Azzi said, grabbing her stuff.

"Let's just meet here at the end of the day to see what we've come up with," I suggested.

"Ok cool, let me get to Mr. Petty class, y'all know he tripping, trying to lock the door in shit," Zina said, walking off into the crowd of melanated scholar's scurrying to be educated.

When I turned, Azzi was already walking away with the science club. Before I knew it, Neffy was there, right in my face. "You coming to class?" Neffy said, smiling and hooking her arm around mine.

"Yeah, let's go," I said, looking back, then we headed to class.

For the next few weeks, we met every day, working diligently on our project for the upcoming Community Cure Science Fair. Before, during and after school, we worked on designs, marketing ads, and the website for the 5-year campaign. What came to be our most difficult challenge was finding a hemp product manufacturer. Most were located in other countries and charged an arm and a leg for their products. After intense searching, finally, we found a company across seas in India. Though not completely to our liking, we had to start somewhere.

I conjured up design after design of black smiles and pictures of black kids doing epic, unbelievable stuff. Along with that, I also created slogans and designs encouraging people to unify. With only a few days before launch, we had everything set and ready to go. We created a small online buzz, but most of our support came from students at the school who bought into the idea and were willing to support. Walking through the halls, I saw people proudly wearing our shirts that said, "Stronger together!" "All Power to the People."

With launch day closely approaching and numerous friends around school supporting our movement, needless to say, we were nervous, yet excited to embark on something that could change our lives and those around us.

The night before, I raged over designs and marketing material, while Azzi and Zina prepared for the presentation. We stayed up all night, going over an extraneous checklist created by the over-achiever, Azzi! It was her dedication and drive that was going to make this a success.

Next morning, when we arrived at school, teachers and students where showcasing our latest designs, greeting us with the phrase "ALL Power!" That was our top selling shirt.

As I walked through the hall on my way to class, a teacher stopped me and asked, "Hey, you designed the shirts for that project "People-Power-Prosperity" clothing line, correct?" she asked, clutching her lower classman social studies lesson plans.

"Yea, with the help of my team, of course!" I replied.

"Hmm, nice, so tell me, 'All Power', what does that mean? I've been hearing people say it all morning," she said with a concerned face.

"It means All power to the people!" I answered proudly and swiftly.

"Oh! Okay. Well, what type of power are you talking about?" she asked.

"The power to create a way of life that provides peace of mind to the People," I responded with a smile.

She sucked her lips in and folded her arms then inquired, "Who are the People?"

Flustered with her questions and hating undertones, I asked, "What are you afraid of? The wrong people gaining power?"

"Yes, I am. Some people don't know how to treat others once they get it," she replied.

I laughed so hard that it felt like I just finished an ab workout. After catching my breath, I said, "Well, ain't that the truth, let's just hope those that come to power are nothing like those in power now. It could get ugly for a lot of people. Don't you think so?"

"No, absolutely not, that would make you no better than them, 2 wrongs never make a right," she replied.

"That's easily said from that side of the fence. Well, good thing nobody is willingly to stoop that low. The People is a mindset, and clearly, you don't have it. Good day," I said as I began to walk away.

When I hit the corner, I saw Zina pulling the presentation materials out of her locker.

"Zina, you ready to get this bag or nah!" I yelled down the hall.

"Boy, this for the People, we have to go even harder now!" Zina replied, hooking bags of Hemp products on to both shoulders.

I hurried down the hall to help. Relieving her some luggage, I said, "Have you seen any of the other projects we're going against?"

"Nah, I haven't, but I heard a guy from Ritter High was introducing something epic though!" she said, slamming her locker closed.

"Damn, they come hard every year," I said as we headed toward the auditorium where Azzi and everyone else was setting up for their presentations.

Entering the auditorium, I could barely move, the room was bursting at the seams with young scientists, entrepreneurs, engineers, and other innovative thinkers from around the state. Insurmountable positive vibes invaded our souls and our fear of failure turned into an opportunity to shine. We entered the room with our project and our heads high.

"You see Azzi!" Zina said, scanning the room for Azzi's distinctive fro. Navigating our way through the sea of geniuses, we saw a project that found a way to clean the Mississippi, one that turned trash into renewable energy, another absorbed pollutants out of the air, windows and paint that absorbs solar energy and fuels the home, and so much more. It was amazing. As we ventured, I spotted a large group in the front by the stage dancing to the tunes of K.Dot and Cole world. Then out of nowhere, a floating fro entered the scene!

"There she is!" I said, making my way through the human cluster. As we made our way to our area, I could see various students and teachers wearing the hemp threads we created. The feeling of seeing people from all walks of life supporting an idea that was meant to bring the masses together, with one purpose, to create a future and a foundation for future generations to marvel at. That feeling was riveting and profound.

"Azzi!" Zina yelled as we got closer to the vibing crowd of supporters.

She turned around, "Fam Laaay! Hurry up and set up, y'all are behind!" she said, guiding us to the presentation table.

"Aye who are these people, Azzi?" Zina asked, checking out the new and strange faces representing the cause.

"Girl huh?! These our people! The believers and supporters! We need all the believers and active supporters we can get. Better act like they're your distant cousins or something and stop being boogie," Azzi said, clearing the presentation table.

"She ain't lying though, you know how fickle support is. Especially for grassroot companies. Low key, we can't take anyone for granted, we need them all," I said, loading the hemp products on the presentation tables.

"He's not lying!" Azzi confirmed. That's when a judge tapped Azzi on the shoulder and asked, "People, Power, Prosperity? Do you have everything you need? We have your team scheduled to go 3rd."

"Ok great, we're ready! Let's finish setting up team!"

After the first 2 presentations, we were up! With all eyes on us, the tension building, I stepped forward and began with a speech we all loved by Charlie Chaplin.

"I'm sorry, but I don't want to be an emperor. That's not my business. I don't want to rule or conquer anyone. I should like to help everyone if possible - Jew, Gentile - black man - white.

We all want to help one another. Human beings are like that. We want to live by each other's happiness - not by each other's misery. We don't want to hate and despise one another. In this world, there's room for everyone and the good earth is rich and can provide for everyone.

The way of life can be free and beautiful, but we have lost the way. Greed has poisoned men's souls - has barricaded the world with hate - has goose-stepped us into misery and bloodshed. We have developed speed, but we have shut ourselves in. Machinery that gives abundance has left us in want. Our knowledge has made us cynical; our cleverness, hard and unkind. We think too much and feel too little. More than machinery, we need humanity. More than cleverness, we need kindness and gentleness. Without these qualities, life will be violent, and all will be lost.

The aeroplane and the radio have brought us closer together. The very nature of these inventions cries out for the goodness in man - cries for universal brotherhood - for the unity of us all. Even now, my voice is reaching millions throughout the world - millions of despairing men, women, and little children - victims of a system that makes men torture and imprison innocent people. To those who can hear me, I say: 'Do not despair.' The misery that is now upon us is but the passing of greed - the bitterness of men who fear the way of human progress. The hate of men will pass, and dictators die, and the power they took from the people will return to the people. And so long as men die, liberty will never perish.

Soldiers! Don't give yourselves to brutes - men who despise you and enslave you - who regiment your lives - tell you what to do - what to think and what to feel! Who drill you - diet you - treat you like cattle, use you as cannon fodder. Don't give yourselves to these unnatural men - machine men with machine minds and machine hearts! You are not machines! You are not cattle! You are men! You have the love of humanity in your hearts. You don't hate, only the unloved hate - the unloved and the unnatural!

Soldiers! Don't fight for slavery! Fight for liberty! In the seventeenth chapter of St. Luke, it is written the kingdom of God is within man not one man nor a group of men, but in all men! In you! You, the people, have the power - the power to create machines. The power to create happiness! You, the people, have the power to make this life free and beautiful - to make this life a wonderful adventure. Then in the name of democracy - let us use that power - let us all unite. Let us fight for a new world - a decent world that will give men a chance to work - that will give youth a future and old age a security.

By the promise of these things, brutes have risen to power. But they lie! They do not fulfil that promise. They never will! Dictators free themselves but they enslave the people. Now, let us fight to fulfil that promise! Let us fight to free the world - to do away with national barriers - to do away with greed, with hate and intolerance. Let us fight for a world of reason - a world where science and progress will lead to all men's happiness. Soldiers, in the name of democracy, let us unite!

Kiesha, can you hear me? Wherever you are, look up Kiesha. The clouds are lifting! The sun is breaking through! We are coming out of the darkness into the light. We are coming into a new world - a kindlier world, where men will rise above their hate, their greed and their brutality. Look up, Kiesha! The soul of man has been given wings and at last, he is beginning to fly. He is flying into the rainbow - into the light of hope, into the future, the glorious future that belongs to you, to me, and to all of us. Look up, Kiesha... look up!"

When I finished, the crowd erupted with cheers! Azzi and Zina rolled out the diverse selection of everyday items made of Hemp. "Everything you will ever need! Can be made better with hemp!" Azzi said, showcasing the diverse assortment of products. "Now stronger, safer, long-lasting, lighter, and with more personal and worldly benefits!" she continued. With Azzi and Zina holding the attention of the hundreds of on-lookers and judges, we finished the presentation in epic fashion.

Students and adults alike cheered at the idea of all hemp products replacing the old, everyday items. Nobody knew how versatile this easily grown plant was until now. With the judges amazed at the presentation and innovation of Hemp, we felt like we had a legit chance of winning this year's Community Cure Fair.

A weight was lifted as the crowd shifted to the next presentation. As they walked away, Zina uttered, "Aye family, we got this, only God can stop us now!" Azzi and I agreed as we came in for a group hug.

As the crowd shifted, I saw a strike of lighting that lit up the room. Everyone was shocked, wondering the origin of the bolt. We hurried over to see, pushing our way to the front of the crowd. Once there, we saw lighting strike again, indoors, with amazement in our eyes, the dude from Ritter walked from behind a curtain and said, "With only that, we can light the East coast for 7 years. Pure, uncut energy harnessed and distributed to the People! Nothing will be the same, only better! Greater! I would like to introduce you to the first Lighting Thief, the future is here."

We looked on as he captivated the judges and crowd. "Bruh, this negro here?" I said with hating undertones.

"He must be God because he just stopped the hell out of us," Azzi said, chuckling and mocking Zina.

Zina rolled her eyes and walked away. "All bs aside, that's pretty dope, can't even hate. If in the right hands, this could be life changing for many people," I stated.

Lighting Struck again, and the people awed and applauded. Even after it was over, the crowd didn't budge for an hour as hundreds circled the contraption, analyzing its battery and state-of-the-art features. When it was time to vote, most contestants had already packed up, knowing they had no chance. They were right. Dude from Ritter won in a landslide and walked away with a huge check and partnership opportunities from tons of fortune 500 companies.

After the Fair, we went for a bite to eat at our favorite black-owned pizza joint, Master Peezza. As we waited for the infamous deep crust 3-layer veggie pizza, we discussed our unfortunate defeat.

"I still don't know how that dude from Ritter won. I mean I get it, just think other projects came a bit harder," Zina pleaded, sipping her lemon water.

"Girl, that presentation was cold! He made lightning strike indoors. Like, think about that for a second," Azzi replied.

"Right, easy on the salt before you have a stroke, we didn't get the bag but as long as it's helping the people, I'm all for it," I said, joining in the conversation.

"Sounds like y'all should've been on his team!" Zina replied.

"Correction. Sounds like we're on the team of the people. All of this is for our folks now and the future generations. You know this though," I said, correcting her statement.

"By people, we mean all people. Well, at least those that wish for a similar way of life. I guess. Oh! Pizza's coming!" Azzi said, grabbing her fork and knife, anxious to cut thru the one of a kind veggie pizza.

"Ouu, I'm about to smash! Dibbs on leftover crust!" I said, spreading out the plates to everyone.

"Boi, don't nobody want that mess but yo fat self!" Azzi said, scooping up 2 slices.

"I guess, pass me the almond parmesan cheese. Please," Zina said, grabbing a juicy slice of the pie.

I took a big gulp of my pure fruit drink, then grabbed a large slice and took a gapping bit. Munching on the delicious pizza, I paused for a second and yelled, "We lit!" We laughed, enjoying our food and company.

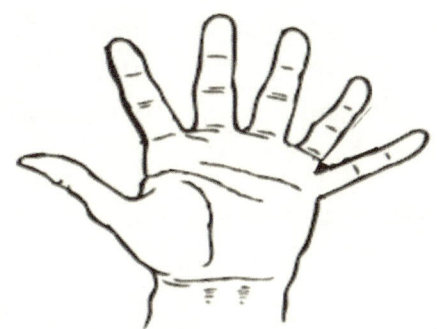

COMMUNITY COME-UP

The next day, I saw Azzi and Zina in the hall. Azzi waved then came to me and asked, "Aye, what you doing after school today?"

I replied, "The same thing I always do, I got to…"

"Boy, you ain't got nothing to do! Come over my crib, Pops need to talk to you. He said bring your thinking cap," Azzi said, cutting me off.

"A thinking cap? Hell he want?" I said nervously.

"Stop being scary, he just wants to talk about the project," she answered.

Still nervous, I agreed to the summons and we all headed there right after school.

When we arrived at the house after school, Selah was already there. "Pops, we're here!" Azzi screamed as Zina and I walked through the door behind her.

"Dang lil girl, I'm right here! I could hear y'all coming up the street," Selah said, walking out of the kitchen close by.

"So, what's up? You had Azzi come to school and summon us on some topsecret type stuff. Must be important," Zina said, walking in and throwing her stuff on the floor next to the couch, and flopping down.

"My dogs have eaten people for lesser tones than that, you're lucky you're like family," Selah said with a mischievous smirk.

I could somehow tell that behind that smirk, he was dead ass serious. He sat down and said, "Tell me why you wanted to start this business/project. But most importantly, why you chose hemp?"

We sat there, stuck like deer in head lights, "Well, it's for the people, we wanted to create something that cannot only help the community but is also simple to acquire. That's kind of the mission of the fair," Azzi said confidently.

"Who came up with the Hemp idea?" Selah asked.

"Umm, yea Syr, why you choose Hemp?" Azzi said, diverting all attention to me.

"Umm, it covered a lot of things, you can do so much with it, and it's easy to grow. I mean I don't know, should we not have used it or something?" I asked, giving him the best response I could think of on the spot.

"Hemp, it's a powerful resource many know nothing of. From oil to clothing to paper to health solutions. If we, the people, can take over that industry, we can change the dynamic of the economy. The possibilities could be endless. I want to invest in your project, I want to be part of the campaign," Selah said, looking us in the eyes.

Joy filled my body. "Of course! Selah, we'll love to have you on the squad. We could use the help most definitely," I said as Zina and Azzi nodded in agreement.

"Well, welcome to the team, old man!" Azzi yelled as she began to dance.

Selah smiled. With Selah now working with us on the campaign, things were taken to a whole new level, and fast.

Within the first week, Selah called for another meeting, informing us of an interview he scored with the top radio station in the city. We met constantly throughout the week. Our orders were to use the small following we had at school to start a volunteer department. They poured in numbers once we said they get free and discounted merchandise. Selah used his resources, he recruited land owners, tradesmen, and others familiar with his community work.

Though pressed for time, we worked together, hard, and smart. We wanted to make sure our message was simple, concise, and thought provoking. Selah felt it was important to perfect our marketing strategies for the campaign, even up to the hour before the interview, I recall him saying, "Delivery is everything. We can be promoting the best stuff in the world. If it's not enticing, appropriate but cool, and tangible, I just don't feel like our people will buy in, not for 5 years for dang sure. So, we need to be on point! We have to bring forth the energy people need to spring into action," he pleaded as he paced back and forth.

"Pops, we'll be good, proper preparation prevents piss poor performance, and we've prepared! Now it's time to practice poise and execute. We got this!" Azzi said, cutting the tension in half, visibly relaxing her father's nerves.

Zina and I sat, patiently waiting, while focusing on our opportunity to share a culture changing idea to the masses. That's when a knock on the door alerted us.

It opened and a slender, white woman entered and informed us that the set was ready. With time closely approaching, we meditated on our mission, then headed out the door of the dressing room.

"In other news, girl, your hair though. You got fine as hell to be on the radio, didn't you!?" Zina said, complimenting Azzi's flowing shinning fro.

"Who me? Thanks girl, you know I have to stay picture-ready in these moments. But for real though, let's talk about all that black girl magic you oozing on everybody!" Azzi replied.

"I slay, we know this," Zina responded with a big smile. The team entered the studio like a lion pride, strong and confident. After a brief rundown of the show, the host was ready to begin.

The radio host counted down, "3, 2,…" then began, "What's up STL! This is your Fav afternoon mixer, Dj SideSwitcher! Here with Education Guru and Community Leader, Selah and The People Power Prosperity Campaign! So, tell us, what's up!?"

"Greeting Family! We're here today to tell you about the next major culture move. This could be our cotton, our gold, our oil, our vibranium. It's hemp! One of the most useful resources our earth has to offer. This is our opportunity to head the industry, as a community, as a culture. We've created an innovative, state-of-the-art company and campaign, structured to pour money back into our own neighborhoods. To fix the issues that we collectively deem imperative," Selah explained.

"Campaign? Tell us what it's all about, brother," DJ SideSwitcher asked.

Selah turned to me. I grabbed the microphone and explained. "In 2 years, our culture amassed over 3 billion dollars in the clothing industry alone. Picture if all that currency went back into our communities. Our communities only need a portion to be able to create, build, innovate and bring our living spaces to the luster it deserves. Our plan is to embark on a 5-year campaign, motivating the masses to buy these fly one of a kind clothing and eventually, other materials from us. If this happens, along with tons of community sweat equality, we can gather enough resources to secure a prosperous sustainable future for the people of St. Louis and other cities alike."

"WOW! That is huge! First, you help rebrand and restructure schools, then you clean up our streets, now you're creating a community industry it sounds like. How will the community be a part of the production process though?" the Dj continued.

Azzi chimmed in, "I'm glad you asked! We, along with some of our partners, have acquired acres of vacant lots and properties around the city. That is not including the many residents that have signed up to be producers, using their lands and backyards to cultivate the hemp plant. Property owners can harvest the crop and bring it to us or trained volunteers will schedule a time to pick up the crop. With enough help, we can produce hundreds of different kinds of hemp products from gas to bricks. By making the community a part of the industry, it gives them the power and motivation to make it an epic success. I think we have slaved for everyone else! It's time we work for ourselves. This is the first step to creating the economic peace of mind we long for."

I quickly got the urge to stand up to applaud but when I started to stand, Zina snatched me back down by the shirt, reminding me where we were.

"Oh ok, sounds like you guys have everything mapped out perfectly! All we have to do is get on board people! I'm going to get me a garden in my backyard for sure! Hold up! How do the people get the garden though?" DJ Sideswitcher asked.

"We give out seeds after our How to Harvest Hemp Seminar. We teach you everything you need to know!" Azzi said quickly.

Selah looked at her with a side eye in confusion.

"They really just making this shit up. Huh," I leaned over and whispered to Zina.

"No, they're freestyling, get it right. Plus, everything starts somewhere. Remember, sparks can turn into forest fires. Mustard seeds turn into trees, so we can change the world. Send a mass text to some of our friends, we're going to need those volunteers," Zina replied, still glued to the conversation as the interview continued.

"Oh okay, great! So, who is the founder, the face, the leader of the campaign?" Dj asked, moving to the next question.

"We are a collective, there is no leader, just we, the people and our idea of a prosperous future," Selah answered.

"No leader? There has to be somebody! Arguments and clashing must be rampant in your meetings. Was not having a leader, a CEO, a collective decision as well?" the disc jockey chuckled though confused and baffled.

"We all agreed this method would work best for the people and this project. When it comes to single leader structures, we've been let down and finessed too often. It's easily dismantled, and one person can quickly be discredited or buried. We don't need a leader, we need a united idea, a mission, a goal, coupled with conviction, faith, and we have that," Selah answered.

"So, what's the goal of this seemingly complex project that requires so much from the people?" DJ asked.

"The goal is simple. It's to create a unified front across this nation. While giving its people the power to control a resource that crosses all human need industries. In all, to create a solid foundation for a sustainable, yet profitable lifestyle for the people for many generations to come," Selah replied.

There was no lie in Selah's statements. That has always been his and our ultimate goal. To educate and create a foundation of peace, ethics, and useful resources to the people who longed for a better way of life. As Selah continued and wrapped up the interview, we already began receiving texts and notifications in support.

"Oh snap, we already popping from the interview!" Zina said as we left the radio station.

"That must mean we did well?' Selah suggested.

"Let's hope so!" Azzi said.

"Man, y'all killed it! I dang near started clapping when you were talking. The message is out, now we just have to do the work and be ready for the people to come!" I said in excitement, proud of my team.

"Word, you're right, now it's time to put in the work!" Selah replied.

We headed back to the lab to cross some T's, dot some I's, and paint all the edges of the picture. For we knew the devil was in the details.

We decided it would be the perfect time to have a launch party for the public. We all agreed to throw a concert showcasing artists from around the city. With the intentions of getting the old and young generations of the city on board with the project. We invited our friends from school and Selah invited numerous community leaders and members. It was going to be epic.

The highly anticipated event came quickly. With the buzz around the city, it was sure to be a success. Azzi, Zina, and I became popular overnight seemingly, drawing tons of posts and requests on social media. Azzi and Zina took full advantage, allowing admirers to buy them lunch every day at school. Though it felt like I was getting more attention, I still found myself alone when I wasn't with Azzi, Zina, or Selah. I had friends, well, rather associates, and though the girls called me lame for always being MIA, I knew I had my reasons, my upbringing had taught me different. If the ones that claimed to love me never accepted me, why would anyone else. At school, random people began speaking and sitting with us at lunch. We didn't mind, unless they were eating pork or smacked when they ate. Azzi and Zina made that very clear.

The day before the concert, Azzi and I went to one of the last malls around to hand out some more flyers. It was packed as usual. With merchants throwing different overpriced items in our faces, we quickly hurried and passed out as many as we could. Azzi joked that the only reason so many women willingly took our flyers was because I was cute. Though I did receive a lot of dreamy eyes and smiles, I felt my energy and spill is what got their attention. After all, I worked on my pitch all night, and I thought it was pretty good. As we made our way through the mall, Azzi pointed out another woman saying, "What you think about her? She cute."

Not noticing her, I turned to take a respectful glimpse then said, "Eh, she cool."

"She thick though!" Azzi said, seemingly surprised by my response.

"So, what you want to turn around and give her a medal?" I replied sarcastically.

She rolled her eyes. "Don't act like that. I'm just trying put you on! I can't have my brother out here lonely!" she said, laughing and then pointed to another, then another.

I had known Azzi for a long time now, I guess I should've been happier to be considered family by her.

We continued through, still handing out flyers to those in our path. She always did this whenever we were around women. Like it was her responsibility to play match maker with me. My responses were always the same, but that never stopped her from trying.

Then Azzi said, "Look at her, now she fine! You can't even hate! And she look like she got that bag."

I looked over at the tall stallion of a woman, walking gracefully through the thick crowd, sundress hugging her frames cleavages front and back. Chin high, with her fro painting the faces of those who walked too close with natural oils and juices. It just looked like she smelled good.

"Dang boy! You look like you seen a dream! Gone get on her then. If you want," Azzi said, stopping me and looking into my eyes.

I looked back, not knowing how to feel. "What you waiting on boy? Hurry so we can finish passing out these flyers," Azzi said.

Though this walking specimen of a woman fit all the physical requirements of any man, I still had no urge to pursue. What was I

115 | C a t t l e   o f   K i n g s

waiting for? Who was I waiting for? I was tired of being the lonely, handsome, quiet friend. I turned and saw the woman getting further and further away. I took one last look at Azzi, then turned in pursuit of the woman.

Moving through the crowd with the determination of a strip club bouncer, who just saw some clown take money off stage, I quickly caught up with her. I saw her aiming toward the entrance of 'Nadheera's Secret', a book and lingerie store. I hurried and just in time, opened the door for her, smiling from ear to ear, trying to make eye contact.

She turned and with a short glimpse said, "Thank you" and walked in without skipping a beat. I looked back, only to see Azzi not insight. I followed her in.

Out of place, but seemingly unnoticed, I followed her to the book section where she had already grabbed a *"Know Your Worth Magazine"* and began paroozing. That's when I realized I had no idea what to say. I stood there, awkwardly looking through women magazines and books.

Starting to feel the tension building, I finally said, "Excuse me, but I just wanted to say, you're a walking work of art. I mean you really floated your way through the mall like a leaf in a warm breeze. I just want to know if that breeze can guide you to my launch party tomorrow. Your attendance will be a blessing." She looked at me and closed her magazine, revealing a magnetic smile.

"All of that for a party invitation, huh? You're way too cute, thank you, I'm Zarolah by the way, you can call me Za," she said, smiling and reaching out her hand.

"I'm Syr and I'm so glad I had the guts to come speak to you, Za," I said, grabbing her hand and flirting with the thought of kissing it.

"So, I should expect for you to be there tomorrow, right? It's going to be a time I know you'll enjoy," I continued, still holding her hand.

"Yea, I'll be there. I look forward to it," she said, letting go and walking away with the flyer.

I stood there, watching the orchestra of movements of her body as she walked away. Snapping out of the daze, I turned and jetted out of the store, feeling accomplished, even though I didn't get her number.

Making my way through the crowd, looking for Azzi, I spotted her at the food court stuffing her face with a huge salad. I made my way to her and sat down. With a mouth full of leaves and grass, she asked, "Well, did you get those digits or nah?"

I smiled and leaned back then replied, "Nah, I didn't, but she'll be at the launch party tomorrow."

"You did all that just to give her a flyer? What you say?" she asked.

"I mean we just talked, and I invited her. I mean, I probably could've gotten her number if I asked for it," I said confidently, taking a swig of her drink.

"You didn't even ask? You hella scary. She probably like, 'if this lil boy don't get on somewhere!'" Azzi said, laughing and pitching the rest of her salad into the bio-waste bin.

"Damn, you weren't going to offer me none before you threw it away? I'm hungry as hell," I said, confused and obviously hangry.

She grabbed her bag and the rest of the flyers then said, "Salads are for winners only fam, sorry. Let's leave this place."

I laughed and replied, "Woooow, that's what we're on? Ok." We set the rest of the flyers in a shoe store and left the mall.

The next day, after spending the morning setting up the venue, we planned to meet at Selah's later that night. When we finished setting up, I shot home to get ready. Though most of my wardrobe was hand-me-down gear from my brothers, I got creative, and always seem to make it work. One thing I had to learn is that it's not what you wear, but how you wear it. With Masego and Coltrain type vibes lowly playing on my phone as I bathed, I soaked and thought of the dope night ahead. When I got done oiling my hair and brushing my teeth, I headed back to my room to get dressed. I dug in the closet and grabbed my favorite pair of black jeans. My favorite because they were my only. A hand-me-down pair of levis from my heavier, older brother, Charles. I never wore them because they were too baggy. Needing them for this outfit, I put them on and put safety pins in the seams to measure off leftover space. I grabbed the needle and thread, took the jeans off, turned them inside out and sewed a seam. Learning from my home economics class, it took no time. To give them a new look, I got a cheese grater from the kitchen and ran it across the legs a few times, then put it back. 'Perfect'. I grabbed a pair of vintage Jordans that I haven't worn in ages from deep down in my closet. Feeling too small, after I scrubbed them down to a new shine, I took the sole out for an extra centimeter or two. I grabbed my favorite shirt from the product line, though it didn't match perfectly, it would work in the dark. Threw my hair in a bun, oiled my flesh, grabbed my bag and headed to the door.

"Where you think you're going?" a voice said from behind me. It was my uncle. I told him weeks ago of the interview and launch party. There was even a flyer on his desk.

"Tonight is the launch party, I'm going over Selah's. We're all going together," I answered. "Who said you can go to this?" he replied with a straight face.

"I told you about this about a week ago or so when we organized it. I even gave you a flyer," I pleaded, too familiar with the outcome of these conversations.

"Syr, I'm sure they're not going to miss their hype man, you need to be here trying to figure out what you want to do with your life. Not hanging out late with some fast, little girls. Doing God knows what," he said staring me down. Before I could reply, he looked down at my jeans then said, "And you're not leaving my house looking like a Mississippi bum. Why does your jeans look like that anyway?"

"I made them like this," I replied.

"It looks like it, let me find out you're using my stuff to cut up your silly ass jeans. Go sit down and turn off the light. Hold up, look at me, you got something you want to say to me. Say it! Say it!" he said, walking towards me. "Like I thought. Dummy." he said, walking away into the next room.

I stood there, frozen in anger, too old for tears, my eyes just watered. Thoughts filled my brain until I blurred out, "I'm leaving, do as you wish."

I grabbed my bag and walked out of the door, then headed down the street. I could hear him kicking me out and cursing me to the bottom of the hottest hells. Reminding me I would be no better that my troubled parents and siblings. I put my headphones in and

119 | C a t t l e o f K i n g s

turned up 'Get Rich or Die Tryin' and let it ride as I walked the dark cuts to Azzi's house. As I walked, all I tried to think about is the opportunity ahead to not only change my life, but most importantly, benefit the community. This was the start of something big. I could feel it, and I was all in with or without his support. I was ready to endure the consequences of my actions. There was no turning back now.

When I finally made it to Selah's, I could hear them joking and laughing from outside. I longed for that noise, the noise of fun and happiness. I knocked, and the door instantly opened. "Fam laaaaay!" Selah said as the door swung open.

"Fam laaay!" I replied.

"I see you with the J's on! What you know about them? You probably wasn't even alive when he was playing!" Selah said, joking.

"You're just hating because hoopers only wore Chucks and Stacy Adams in your day," I replied, pointing at his opened toe crocs. Azzi and Zina, sitting on the couch started laughing. I looked over and noticed they weren't even ready yet. "What, y'all want to get there at the last minute or something? This is not a regular club night where we can show up an hour before it closes, this is our event," I said, staring at them as they lounged and picked at their nails.

"Boy listen, we got this! The spot is already set up, volunteers know the spill and are working the stands and door. Plus, Azzi got us a fine DJ to keep everyone busy until we get there," Zina explained.

"Then all we do is cut the bow and have some fun!" Azzi added.

Selah walked over and butted in, "Umm, actually. We have interviews and major networking to do tonight. This is work for us still until we reach our goal. Remember that. With that said, it's always good to make an entrance and most definitely, a crime not to have fun. Azzi, turn the music back up."

Azzi hit the volume to the music and we all began to dance and laugh. The girls took their time getting ready as usual. While they did, Selah and I sat in his den. I looked through all the pictures and prizes he's won over the years. He'd done so much for the people. He could stop now and still be remembered forever, or at least, get a street named after him.

"You gone top all this, lil King?" he asked.

"Top it? I'm going to have a room like this the size of y'all backyard!" I replied enthusiastically.

"I'm sure, it's something about you that silently screams leader, fighter, a story, and purpose. Those kinds of people always have rooms like this. Many don't get a chance to see them, so feel special," he said, sitting down and pouring himself a drink. "Come have a seat," he insisted.

I walked over to the couch and sat down. "So, what's up with you and my daughter? Be real with me, this is your only chance," he said, sipping his drink and folding his legs.

I froze, shocked from the bluntness of the question, I stumbled and said, "Umm, nothing's up. She's been my friend since we were little. Y'all are like family to me."

He sat right there, looking at me, as if he was waiting to see if I cracked a sign of deceit. "I'm going to let you think about that," he said, standing and walking over to a samurai sword posted on the wall.

I hurried and replied, "I'm not lying. I wouldn't even lie if I was on that with her because I would respect her, and you'll be the first to know. She calls me brother! I couldn't get her if I wanted. I've been 'bro-zoned' for years!"

Selah took the sleeve off the sword. I stood up just in case I had to do some parkour moves to get to the door. But he immediately told me to sit down. His 6'8 frame and black belts hanging from the wall convinced me to sit down, and at least, hear the man out.

"So why is my daughter crying over you?" he said, walking slowly toward me. I stood up again and he said, "You won't make it!" I sat back down and thought, what could he be talking about and my memory only drew blanks.

I looked at him cluelessly, frustrated and honestly professed, "I do not know nothing about what you're talking about, Selah. This is news to me. I'm not about to let you corner and threaten my life like this though. When you can just tell me what's up."

Selah looked at me and grinned and said, "That's why I like you, my bad, Syr. I just overheard them in the room talking about how you left her for some older fine woman in the mall and she was crying. So, what's up?"

I leaned back in the chair in astonishment and said, "Wow, she told me to get on her, she pointed her out, I wasn't even paying attention until she said something. She always hoeing me off to women she thinks are good fit for me. Saying she can't have her brother out here lonely. This time, I actually saw one I liked. I'm confused."

When I finished, Selah held a smirk then said, "Boy, y'all young as hell and need to stop. Now that you know that my daughter was crying, it should be common sense how she feels. It's up to you to use this information wisely to pursue or perish. I'll let y'all figure out the rest for now."

I sat there, silently thinking of what all this could mean. He took another sip of his drink then continued, "If you're going to be around my daughter, you have the responsibility to protect her, and always offer her the best you. Cherish every moment making as many memories as you can of laughter and joy. Be sure, be real, and innerstand she's human too. In this realm, our time is limited, so don't waste yours, hers or anybodies for that matter. When you find that one that matches your soul across dimensions, you love her and fight to see that smile every day," he said, pulling out a picture from his inner pocket and gazing deeply into it as if he was thanking every spec of ink that created this figure. Could it be his deceased wife? When we were little, Azzi told me she had been captured during a civil war in Africa and was never seen again. Shortly after, Selah and Azzi came to the US. Azzi told me stories of her mother's strength and intelligence. How she led her country to a better day and fought against oppressors. Azzi spoke of her as if she was a legend. I could only imagine how Selah felt for her then and hurt for her now. Abruptly snapping out of his daze, Selah said, "They should be ready, we should be heading out soon. Tell them to be at the car in 5 minutes." I nodded my head then walked out the door and did just that.

When we got to the car, everyone was laughing and joking except me. I still had Selah's words on the mind. Does Azzi like me or something? I thought. Thinking of the admiration from someone I had found to be the most beautiful creation sent chills through my body. But she was always trying to put me on girls and calling me bro? Confusion filled my mind. Before I could get into the car, Selah stopped me. "Aye, your attitude is lukewarm as hell right now. I know you got things on your mind now, but you need to snap out of it. We have a mission, so all of us are going to need you to be on point. Never forget why we're doing this," he uttered low but sternly.

"Oh, I'm good. I was thinking about something random, that's all," I replied, lying and then getting in the truck.

Once in, Azzi and Zina was dancing and singing the booty tunes on the radio. "They ain't saying a word that makes sense, but this go hard!" Azzi said, grooving.

"If it did makes sense, it'll probably still be degrading," Zina replied, jigging in the backseat.

"It doesn't matter, y'all are still going to dance anyway," I said.

Selah jumped in the driver seat, turned it down and said, "It's the drums and melody. You can say just about anything over a nice baseline, chorus, and melody. People just don't know it's being used against us. Always have and always will be as long as we let it."

Azzi leaned back in the seat, took a deep sigh, and mumbled, "Here he goes about the effects of auto suggestion again." Like she has heard this lecture many times before.

"Don't worry, I'll shut up. But am I lying though?" Selah concluded, turning the booty tunes back up to a reasonable volume. From the backseat, I could see her still grooving as the night sky and passing street lights danced off her radiant flesh as we drove through the city.

Arriving, the cars were packed in and the line was wrapped around the block. My heart dropped as we drove pass the eager patrons. So many people from all over that I've never seen before coming to support our cause. We parked upfront and walked right in, following the lead of Selah. Entering the club, Selah and Azzi instantly began to receive love and hugs from numerous people. We slowly navigated through the crowd, greeting our people joyously, on our way to our prepared section. Zina and I just followed. With the music playing and so many positive vibes around, this was already turning into a great night.

They knew so many people, guys and girls from all colors and backgrounds. I never made it past greetings before I wrote people off. It was normal for me, to stay in my square, safe where nobody could hurt or see the pain that was already there. That was my norm for so long, but that Syr had to come to an end. I had done too much to get to this party, I wasn't going to spend it watching everyone else have fun, I was going to make the best of it.

With the team already working the room, I jumped from the safety of the private section and began to mingle. I figured if I walked up smiling then gave a compliment, or noticed something small and gave it positive light, people would talk. Soon, I was starting random conversations with people and dancing with willing participants. It didn't take long before I was having a blast. It was like all of my troubles had moved down the line, and my happiness was on deck. Azzi and Zina continued to network as Selah talked business with the potential investors in attendance. So, I followed and did the same.

While having small talk with a new investor, I noticed a split forming in the club crowd, a curvy figure appeared. Dancing majestically to the vibrations, the rhythm hypnotized her body, popping, swaying, to the song like a goddess of movement. I looked at her from her toes to her head. It was Azzi coming right towards me. She lassoed me with seductive eyes and a gesture to come to her. I immediately halted the conversation and walked to her. She gazed into my eyes and bit her lip. In awe of such a gesture,

I began to blush. She walked over to me and grabbed my hands while still dancing. Then out of nowhere, she burst into laughter, saying, "Boy, I'm just playing! What you over here doing?" I stood there, still in a daze from the spell just put on me. Usually, I would just play it off and laugh but this time was different.

I looked her up and down, still holding her hand. She looked back at me, smiling and then said, "Why you looking like that creeper? Come on, let's go get some smoothies!"

Not knowing how to feel, I just began to laugh and followed, saying, "What, you reading my mind now? I was just about to go get one too."

We made our way to the fruit bar then ordered. While waiting on our double order of Freaky Berries, a non-alcoholic fruit smoothie, she said, "I'm surprised these girls aren't all over you! You ain't out here recruiting no baddies tonight?"

I gave her the stale face as she giggled. With the drinks on the way, I leaned over and said, "Actually, I'm sitting next to the baddest thing in the building."

She turned to me, smiling and said, "Awe, thank you!" I grabbed the drinks and tipped the fruitender. She sipped her smoothie then checked her phone. She grinned, closed her phone then said, "You gone be right here? I'm about to run upstairs real fast."

With a mouth full of different flavored berries, I nodded in agreement. With smoothie in hand, she disappeared into the crowd. I sat, listening to the live music, occasionally looking over the heads of the crowd to see if I could spot her returning.

Taking a sip of the smoothie, I felt a soft touch from my shoulder to the back of my neck. I turned to see who was responsible for such a pleasurable touch. "Za!" I said, shocked.

She moved around and sat down. She was wearing skin tight jeans and over them hung my favorite sweater, 'If I can't build with you, I can't chill with you', it read. Glowing and smiling, showing all her pearly white teeth, she asked, "You look surprised, is everything ok?!"

"Yea, I'm good! I'm so happy you could make it!" I replied, looking around for Azzi. I finally spotted her standing at the top of the steps, looking right at me. I held my arms up as if to guide her to me. She stood for a few more seconds then turned around and walked away.

I looked at Za and said, "Can you wait right here, one of my business partners need me." I stood and made my way through the vibing crowd and headed upstairs. Once at the top, an odd feeling took over me. My heart dropped. Azzi, head buried on his chest, she was already hugged up with the DJ, and he was taking a big ol' swig of the smoothie I just bought for her. She turned and spotted me. Hugging his arm tighter, she turned away as if I was never there. I was hurt.

I took one step in rage with the urge to shove that drink down his throat. Then I took three steps back in understanding, then headed back down the steps. I made it back to the bar where Za was still waiting. I sat back down and apologized for the delay.

She looked at me and said, "Are you sure you're ok? It looks like the project launch is going as planned! It's so many people here! You should be celebrating!"

I looked back up the steps, then looked back at her then said, "I'm celebrating, I'm celebrating with you and this Goddess ora you brought in with you. I'm so glad you came so I could get a chance to put my eyes on you again."

She cracked a smile, rubbing her neck and ear, she replied, "Wow, um thank you, Syr! Your game is tight, young man."

I moved closer then said, "I mean, I just see something different in you, I'm just hoping you give me the chance to see what that may be."

She smiled, silently inspecting my build, up then down. I was digging her, and she was feeling me. Our vibes flowed smooth, heightening each other's presence. Lingering in tasteful company, we talked and laughed as many songs went ignored.

When there was finally a pause in the enticing dialog, she leaned over and asked, "Can you leave for a second, or do you have to stay?"

I looked around, spotting Selah and Xho in the corner lounge still doing interviews and taking pictures with his balling investor friends. I looked at the top of those steps one last time to only see strangers. I stood up, grabbed her hand and said, "Yea, we can roll." She stood up and we headed for the front door.

Walking into the cool night, she pulled me to her car up the street. "This all you?" I said.

It lit up as she unlocked and automatically started the car.

"Who else will it be silly?" she replied with a sarcastic smile.

Once in the car, I asked, "So where you taking me gorgeous?"

She threw the new year Tesla in drive and skurted off down the street. "You ever been to the latest exhibit at the old art wall? I want to show you something," she said, cracking the windows and turning up 'Yeonce.

"Nah, but I'm down to see what you're trying to show me," I replied, leaning my seat back. We drove under the night sky, headed downtown to the old Art wall. Arriving, I could see the 20-foot tall wall filled with the dynamic street art, created by people from all around the world. It was so amazing. We drove to the top of a hill that overlooked the river.

Now parked, we sat, talking and vibing to some chill-hop and other smooth instrumentals. "So, you seem paid, what is it that you do?" I asked curiously.

"I created, then started minding my own business. Stayed focus and now I have luxuries many don't. I'll just leave it at that," she replied, still bobbing her head to the flow of the music.

Looking and digging her presence, I just smiled and leaned back, enjoying the enchanting scenery. She leaned over and put her hand in my hair and began massaging my head. "Looks like you've had a long day," she implied. Maybe she could see me attempting to shove the day's disappointment out of my head?

"You can tell? What are you trying to say? I'm ugly or something?!" I said, jokingly deflecting and lightening the mood.

"Not at all, it just looks like you need some personal attention," she said, continuing to caress my head then to my neck and shoulders.

My stomach filled with butterflies and the rest of my body covered in goosebumps. Is something about to happen? I asked myself. She was so enchanting, enticing, and most importantly, oddly into me.

Not adept in the field of pleasure, I sat still, wishing she would never stop. She moved her hand from my shoulder to my chest, gently grabbed me by the jaw and placed her lips on mine. Moist, sweet, voluptuous kisses. Her tongue massaged mine. I could feel the blood frantically rushing to my manhood. She moved her hand slowly down my abdomen, until she softly clutched my manhood. Her freshly manicured hands explored my flesh from the crown down, biting my lip as we kissed.

"Umph, I'm going to have some fun with you, all of you," she said, unbuckling my belt.

The pleasure was overwhelming, I could not fight it. I finally cleared my mind. I reached over and pulled her tight frame on top of me. She reclined the seat, then smoothly grasped me by the neck. Gazing off into my eyes with a pure look of lust, she began to grin, unrobing herself slowly with just enough room to insert me into her. Her nectar flowed profusely as her universe hugged me tightly. The stars and moon watched through the panoramic roof. Falling into a spell of pleasure, this became an experience I could never forget.

Intertwining our spirits like the hairs in a loc of an ancestor.

Energies flow deep and deeper in the sacred being of her.

Opening doors and releasing a burst of primal hymbs of pleasure.

More! More! More!

Her temple and mental are deeper than most care to explore,

I plummet to her summit,

More! More! More!

Screamed our spirits as they kissed, each sending us deeper into ecstasy.

Our bodies clutch together, we fit like a piece to a divine puzzle.

Her.

To match with only the righteous for a bond like this

is a bond forever.

When finished, she laid on top of me as we looked over the river at the starry night. We wondered and spoke about the stars and beyond. It was starting to get really late and I knew I still had a lot of people to answer to before it was over. After catching our breath, and getting proper, we headed to the Westside to drop me off. On the way to my side of town, we saw some Community Patrol officers pulled over helping an elderly woman fix a flat tire.

"Man, y'all are so lucky, we did not have this when I was growing up. It was actually frowned upon in the culture," she said, driving by and honking at the officers for doing good work.

"What you mean?" I replied.

She looked at me funny and said, "Just know, snitches got stitches, and nobody most definitely wanted to be Community Patrol Officers. Now people are seeing how well it could work. Selah and Badger really outdid themselves. I know the Police Department had to cut back on officers because of it. Even Xhosah with the Women's Union. She took over the educational system. That's why y'all have the resources to do these fairs and community projects. This generation is blessed."

I agreed but reminded her that we still had some ways to go and many unforeseen obstacles.

She simply looked at me smiling and replied, "As long as you know!"

Pulling up to my house, my heart instantly slowed in depression by the negative energy that lingered inside. I told her to park a few houses down. Once there, she put her hand on my thigh, then said, "Syr, you're a great guy but I want to give you something to remember. Feed your talents often and plenty. Follow your dreams or they'll haunt you and things only work, if you work. And everything you need to change the world is already within you. Figuring those things out saved my life."

Confused where the origin of the statement came from, I replied, "What makes you tell me that?"

She laughed and said, "You're a young black man in America, trying to change it, things can get real. I just want to give you the motivation and reassurance you need to continue to prosper young king! I see a light in you."

I blushed, not knowing how to take it and said, "Thank you." She leaned over and hugged me tightly, then kissed me softly.

"Until next time," I said, exiting the car. Once on the porch, she pulled off and hit her horn.

Still in possession of my house keys, I slowly unlocked the door. As it opened, I could see the flashing dim light of the Tv. He was up. I walked in, drained and ready to endure the consequences of my actions. I locked the door and walked pass the dimly lit front room. I spotted him sitting in the dark corner, staring and me, rotating his half empty glass of yac in his hand. I stood there as the tension built to a breaking point. A breaking point different from the others that exist in the past between him and I. I took a step back, turned and went to bed. He didn't say a word to me that night, or for the next 4 months. Our relationship, or lack thereof, was never the same.

Many things changed after that night. My uncle wasn't the only person not talking to me, though we never really spoke in the first place. With Azzi, we remained cordial but slowly started to become distant. She got a boyfriend and began sitting at another lunch table. At our project meetings, she spent most of her time texting and eating. Only engaging to tell us what she didn't like or wasn't going to do. It seemed like things were going well for the business, but our team was beginning to fall apart. Zina and I remained close, growing our bond even stronger. It seemed like our vibes together never skipped an uplifting beat, no matter the current circumstances.

Following the epic public launch concert, Selah and Xho held in-depth community meetings. With the way it was set up, it was a party, only they discussed ideas and strategies to propel the people. Along with Xho providing various forms of entertainment and a fresh artsy atmosphere, different generations were able to mingle in peace.

The money that was earned from the extravagant events was put into community projects and bigger celebrations for the people. With so much local support, it wasn't long before people started requesting plots and plots of the dynamic crop. Our team was getting bigger and stronger, but Selah stood at the head of the project. He took on the major task, organizing the plans and meetings. Only a matter of time passed before the community named him the leader of the People's Union. Though that was never his objective, he took the role to heart and charged full steam ahead.

The People's Union was working in full force with Selah at the lead. Volunteer tradesmen in the union worked out a plan to work only one project at a time and only give each worker a 10-hour a month responsibility. Even with all of that, it was a struggle at first. To begin, we worked with only 50 consistent volunteers. It wasn't until after a campaign called, "Get Your 10 In" that many more people began to flow in. It asked people of the unions and in the community to do 10 hours of community service a month, working on crops, solar & bio-waste management, fixing homes, or teaching at the schools. You could simply donate $10 to the cause as well. Community members that got the most hours and finished the most projects got nice perks from local businesses and the unions. Soon, it became a pass time for some.

The concrete made from the hemp grown in the neighborhoods, was used to rebuild a few homes, buildings, and pave ruined roads. With many of the cities' structures being built in the 1800s with toxic materials and hardly kept up over the years, many community members praised and embraced the needed makeover. Money earned from the drop shipment of clothes bought bio-waste containers and solar panels for a few poorly funded schools. Though the at-need school list was around the block, it was a start. Though we had tremendous local success, we knew deep down the buzz didn't catch on like we thought and knew the risk of people falling off the wave was very real.

LOST CAUSE

ehind closed doors, though it seemed to be a small rift forming between Azzi and I, our products were selling like crack in the 80's. You could go into any school in the city and find at least a few students proudly representing the brand. You could go into any community and witness our crop cultivated and used. We were exporting shipment after shipment of crop to our chosen hemp paper and concrete manufacture in Illinois. Things were coming together, leaving everyone hopeful. Though I always smiled and played things off, I secretly really missed my old friend.

As time passed, I began to feel our bond slip though we pretended otherwise for face value often. Caleb, "The Dj", Azzi's boyfriend, made his presence felt in the household, often sitting in on meetings. I pretended to be happy and supportive, but my disdain for their union bled deep within me. To dull the pain, I drenched myself in the company of Za. She was different, ostentatious, yet mysterious. Our conversations often drifted to money, passion, travel, or fashion. All led to her inviting me into her body. Though we couldn't hangout much because of her work schedule, when we did, it was fun. Time passed smoothly.

It was a humid but a gloomy summer day in the Lou. The team was returning to Selah's house after our monthly meeting with our top community growers. As we came rolling down Goodfellow Ave, Selah's phone rang. "Answer," he said, linking his phone to the truck's stereo.

"Hello! Hello! Selah?!" the caller said frantically.

"Hello?! What's going on!" Selah replied.

"The cops are trying to destroy the crops!" the caller yelled over the screams and noise in his background.

"What?! What are you talking about?! Where are you?!" Selah said, pulling the truck over.

"Cops are raiding and spraying chemicals all over the crops in The Grove! We need back up or we're going to lose everything!" the caller replied.

Selah hung up then slammed on the gas and hit a U-turn. Just like that, the energy flipped, and we were headed towards the Grove neighborhood! Flying down the street, Selah ordered Azzi to call The PPC and tell them to meet us in The Grove with as many men as he could bring.

We blazed through light after light, headed South. Selah's phone was ringing off the hook from growers in the area looking for answers. When we pulled up, cops were everywhere, spraying large unmarked bottles of chemicals on the private crops of residents.

Some community members watched while others fought for the land in desperation. Selah told us to stay put and jumped out of the car. He covered his face then ran to the nearest house with a garden. With no weapons, he began to protect it from cops, keeping them off the yard. Residents came from their homes to join him in protecting the land.

"We have to help him! We just can't stand here and watch!" Azzi pleaded as we witnessed the chaos. "I have to help my father!" Azzi continued as she opened the door and entered the war-like zone.

With no hesitation, Zina and I followed closely. Stepping into the mayhem, we were instantly welcomed by the sting of pepper spray and the confusion of hundreds of screaming residents. We pushed through the crowd until we got to Selah. We got the residents and community members to lock arms and stand firm to protect the remaining homes and crops. That's when a line of black SUVs broke the horizon, heading our way.

Roaring down the avenue, honking their horns, the parade of black trucks cleared the streets until they came to a screeching stop right in front of us. It was The PPC and other people willing to defend! A slew of armed men of all races exited the vehicles and took post around the residents and Selah, keeping the hazmat officers at bay. A general ran to the front of the crowd with his deep raspy voice. He yelled into the bullhorn, "STAND FIRM!" The line of protectors and residents grew thicker and bigger.

"Record! Call the media so the people can see what they are doing to us!" one resident yelled and demanded.

Cops and hazmat officers made threats to use gun fire and the harmful chemicals to clear the area. But the crowd stood strong, withstanding the unjust treatment like the ground on the path of a herd of Bison.

The intense standoff went on for several minutes before news crews arrived. Once spotted, many officers retreated, dodging interviews and questions. Once the last police vehicle pulled off in a frenzy, the line relaxed. The devastation they left in their tracks stretched for blocks. Ruined crops covered in orange chemicals, destroyed bio-waste containers, and broken solar panels riddled the streets. The devilish deed left families hysterical, discouraged, and distraught. That was only the beginning.

Over the next 3 days, crops and most of the energy advancements made throughout the city, had been dismantled. Some were burned down or dug up by renegade Alt right defenders, while other residents took it upon themselves to rid their property of the new-found burden. The tide had turned, the vibes around the city were mixed, but all were filled with disgust. Some wanted Selah to pay for the damage to their property, some went under the wing of the police and local government, many moved away, others, like Selah, felt it would be the perfect time for the people to unite, and fight for peace and stability. Selah understood that the alt right ideology was the secret spirit and foundation of the government. So, he knew, like always there would be no justice from them. Not after what he was trying to do.

With the news now out about the tragedy, many people were looking to Selah for answers. Though the people in the community knew what happened, the headlines around the country read, *"Drug Addicted neighborhood Raided! Police met by thugs!"* *"Sanctions stop Community Come Up!"* *"Feds Fry Funky Farms In St. Louis neighborhood!"* *"Garden Gangsters are in deep fertilizer!"* and so on. Only no stations had spoken with Selah, or anyone from the community. While everyone was in a panic, looking for answers, Selah had been working diligently on rebuilding the property loss in the raid. It wasn't until he was approached by a local black news company that he agreed to share his thoughts on the city's recent events.

The day was hot and breezy when the interview was released. As soon as it hit the shelves, word spread around the city. Though Selah answered many questions, the only one printed was, "Selah, who are the people against, what are you fighting to achieve?" In the article, Selah's answer painted a picture for the masses, one he hoped they would remember for years to come. When the reporter asked the question, Selah replied, "It doesn't have to be like this. I am not against a person, a set of people, color, or political side. I am against a destructive way of life. Where war is the answer, our solution to school shooting is giving untrained, underpaid teachers guns. A way of life that makes you not love who you are. A way of life where people get paid for you to hate, kill, oppress each other. Our leaders spew divisive speech, our role models are criminals and junkies, so we're showed. We teach our children lies and folktale then swear it's truth. We have drugs and prison instead of cures and therapy. Greed will have our land bare, water toxic, and skies black. Murderous wars are raged over useless materials and things that kill people, innocent people, and children! A way of life that is anti-life, anti-freedom, anti-peace. That's what I'm against! I just want people to think and realize, it doesn't have to be this way. The good must take over. To ensure that in the event that this country does end its toxic relationship with the people. The people need a healthy foundation built on righteous ethics, and a system built on peace, prosperity, and longevity. We must stop waiting for the few to give the many, the permission to live, love, explore, unite, and grow pass their comfort zones."

With the article now released and instantly viral, the people embraced Selah everywhere he went. Random community members would give him hugs and food. Though he didn't always eat the food, he did provide everyone with warm hugs and a huge smile. The People's Union worked hard to bring the Grove community back to its original luster and most of the work was complete.

A week or so after the attack, a woman in the grocery store began to vomit blood, and was rushed in to the E.R. Her results showed she'd been ill due to poison from a toxic chemical. Before the week ended, over 70 similar cases surfaced. All in the same neighborhood. Once Selah got wind of the first few, he immediately told people to stop drinking the water. He called and spoke with newspapers, news and radio stations but none released a story. With nowhere to turn to spread the news quickly to the masses. Selah called on The People's Union who went from house to house in the Grove community, spreading the word. We covered the entire neighborhood in only a matter of hours. With the People's Union now on high alert, we were able to get 55 off duty nurses to patrol the neighborhood, checking on residents showing signs of illness. Local plumbers and scientists checked the pipes and cut off the water, to look for the origin of the sickness. The community searched and waited for answers to what was making everyone ill. One evening, when a patrolling nurse visited Ms. Harriet, an elder community member, she found a private property surveillance camera overlooking the park. The nurse asked to see it and found out that the tape hadn't been viewed in years. Once investigated, the video displayed one of the most atrocious acts seen in the city. The video showed the day of the attack, policemen and hazmat officers pouring the toxic chemicals used to kill the crops into the local sewer/water system. Though many had already assumed the news, it sent a shock wave of panic around the city. Instantly, attacks and vandalism against law enforcement ensued. But we had another issue, people were becoming sicker and sicker with supplies running out fast. Selah reached out to people all over, to no avail. News stations blocked the stories, papers wouldn't print the chaos, and even social media created algorithms to where people's posts only reached their neighbors it seemed. It was like the Detroit and New Orleans water crisis all over again. The community looked to Selah to fix the issue many believed he created. With donated supplies running low and no signs of help on the way, Selah gathered workers and local investors to help rebuild the damaged properties. Also bringing doctors and nurses to the aid of the sick. Keeping his promise to do what was needed to make the community right again.

Though Selah and his team diligently put the neighborhood back together, residents weren't satisfied and wanted revenge on the city that wronged them repeatedly. He figured with so much tension and momentum in the city, he could use the energy to his advantage.

One night, soon after the attack and interview, Selah devised a plan. His plan was to hit them where it hurts, their pockets. Selah formed a team of his most trusted friends. Everyone was on board.

Once everything and everyone was in place, Selah, with the help of some old friends, found a way to get prisoners state-wide to go on strike from doing corporate labor. Though the media coverage was vague, the people knew what was up. It didn't take long for the stocks to drop drastically. With negotiations going in circles, though they had many demands, the prisoners made the important ones clear; no corporate labor, unless they received the same pay as someone that was free. They wanted contracts with black-owned businesses and local start-ups, life coaches, rehab, and better food. The first phase was going smoothly! Now it was time for the next.

Selah didn't wait long to bring the unions together. All we needed was 3 packs of alka-seltzers and a loud screamer. Unidentified airport employees and a few actors went to work at the airport like a normal day. Once in place, at the same time, but in different parts of the airport, they popped the fizzy pills then fell to the ground, with the order to Harlem shake until the ambulance came. With members drooling and shaking, on que the screamer ran through the halls coughing and screaming, "There's a virus breakout! Everyone get out of here! Now!" Instantly, mayhem ensued. People were running out of the airport through all doors! The media arrived before the cops and it hit the news like a wild fire. Hundreds of inspectors in hazmat suits filled the premises. All planes to and leaving St. Louis stopped for a week, costing millions of dollars and tons of headaches.

Meanwhile, community members working for corporations and businesses that they wanted out of their neighborhood, they simply went to work and stood there. Allowing customers to have a free for all. Though many were fired, others eventually just ended up standing there, because now, the stores were empty. Black workers and other members of the People's Union continued to go to work. With a list of People's union stores equipped to provide all of the things the people need, the economy switch didn't skip a beat. Delivery drivers played a big role in bringing goods to the people while many of the other businesses closed and left town. Salt levels were higher than the Atlantic. But salt only kill snails, not playas.

The strike and bad business removal was going as planned, and money was flowing rapidly to the community and circulating within it. Not to mention the sales from the Hemp gear was on the rise, setting us up for another wave of community improvements. The state did not know what just hit them. They didn't realize, they had only seen a lick compared to the real bite the people had. The people saved their next move for the right time, for it could cause major monetary disfunction to many innocent unwilling participants. The point was made, and disfunction of the innocent was never the goal. Things where looking up for the city of New St. Louis and the people.

With so many good blessings coming our way, Xho knew it was time for a big celebration and community surprise. The team invited bands and artists from around the state, but surprised the people with performances from the light-skinned guy from Canada and more. With everyone dressed to kill, and limos wrapping around the luxury venue, this celebration for the people was bound to be epic. Zina, Za, and I arrived together, draped in matte black. There were hundreds, maybe thousands in attendance from all over. You could hear the amazing music and laughs from outside. Everyone from our team was already there and enjoying themselves. When we walked in, the positive vibes drenched us at the door then flowed us to the area where the team was gathered. Azzi and DJ stood, entertaining the crowd with jokes and humor. Selah and the other OG's circled them with drinks and cigars, enjoying the vibes.

"Zina!! Syr! Bring y'all ass over here and fuck with ya people!" Selah yelled with a cigar and drink in his hands.

"Fam Laaaaay!" I replied with open arms. Everyone turned and looked. Including Azzi, only her smile fled. She sat down and DJ followed.

We greeted everyone with hugs, secret handshakes, and cheek kisses. When I finally got to Azzi, she gave me a fist bump while DJ simply hit me with the head nod. Zina and Za got the same treatment. Confused, I looked at Zina. She shrugged her shoulders.

To break the tension, I asked, "I know I ain't the only one hungry, where the food at?"

DJ replied with a finger pointed to the corner of the room, where tables with hot food lined the wall.

"Bet, anybody want anything?" I said, looking around.

Za and Zina both said, "Yes."

That's when Azzi stood up and said, "Zina, come look at these dope paintings by this artist from KC!"

"Umm, ok, let's go girl, I've been wanting to see some good work for my room," Zina said then looked at me and finished, "Just grab me some chips and water please."

Sensing the awkwardness, I replied, "Ok bet!" then grabbed Za and headed to the food.

"What's up with them?" Za asked me.

"Shit beats me, whatever it is, it ain't got shit to do with us," I replied.

"You right, hope everything good with them," she said as we approached the food tables.

"Yea, me too," I replied.

We grabbed small plates of food, chips and water for Zina then headed to explore the event. Heading out of the private room, we encountered art from over the state, live music and humans mingling without a worry in mind. Za was having a blast as we floated through the venue, spreading and enjoying the magnetic positive vibes. The night was turning out to be one for the books.

While conversing with some community leaders from the south of the state, I turned and noticed a strange man staring into the door way. He was looking into the private room where Selah and the team resided. I looked closer to see if he was a familiar face. He wasn't. Leaving Za behind, I began to approach, that's when he turned and vanished in the crowd. Thinking nothing of it, I returned and continued to enjoy the conversation and atmosphere.

As the night went on, the people and members celebrated freely. Selah, Xho, and some other OGs had something tailor-made for the people, and we thought it would be epic for the city to see. The anticipation fueled anxiety. Finally, it was getting close to the revealing of the community surprise. Members began to coral participants to the stadium room. Selah and the team, though tipsy, headed to the stage to present the gift. Za and I spotted Azzi and Zina, as they finally returned. They had looks of bad breath, presumably because they just spent so much time talking shit about folks, or maybe it was something very serious. I was sure I would find out soon. The seats filled, and the crowd scooched in until they were shoulder to shoulder.

The host ran onto the stage to introduce Selah in front of investors, entrepreneurs, and community members from around the state. As he walked on to the stage, we could hear a silence run over the crowd as Selah approached. Arriving to the stage in very smooth OG fashion, Selah grabbed the mic and said, "Fam laaaay! Before we get started, we just want you to know all of this is for you and the people alike. It will always be about you. Know that!"

The crowd screamed in agreeance with Selah and the mission. The program continued showcasing top Scholar artists and entrepreneurs from all over. Selah smiled and laughed as the crowd cheered on the people. When finished with all the other announcements and awards, enthused, Selah yelled, "Now, it's time for the Community surprise!"

Out of nowhere, Xho rolled a table with a silk cover hiding a bulky object. Selah walked over to the table. He stood in front of the table then said, "Family, I'm happy to announce we will be renovating and using the old JC Penny building on MLK as a hub for new restaurant owners and chefs. Decided on by member votes, it'll be called Cokelys, after the great thinker and researcher, Steve Cokely." He then snatched the black covering off the new state-of-the-art building model. The audience erupted in applause and cheers. Selah continued, "With support for the entire team of participating cooks and restaurants, we will also provide delivery for all stores. Restaurants rotate and switch daily or weekly depending on the buy in from the customers. Once they raise enough money and backing, we will help them get their own store!" The crowd erupted into cheers and screams. Still standing on stage with a smirk, Selah added, "But family, that's not all! Welcome the Greek Coalition! The newest force of the Union!" Hundreds of frat and sorority representatives from across the state walked on stage to show the new alliance with the People's Union. The crowd erupted with excitement of the new collaboration.

Za turned to me and said, "That's big, like real big! Y'all celebrations about to be crazy lit!"

After the new Greek Coalition was introduced a line of young men and women entered the stage. Selah then turned around in excitement and said, "It has taken us awhile to mend ties, and pay off the debts of the drug dealers here in the city. Those that left the game weren't left out to dry. That's not what we're on. So, we transferred their skills and turned them into global tradesmen, marketers, salesmen, and ambassadors for the Union. Filling stores here and abroad with our hemp products and frozen dishes made at Cokelys! Also selling solar tents and biowaste adaptors to at need countries, while teaching them how to cultivate native foods.

But before they are ready, the ambassadors had to pass personality, life & social skills, finance, language, combat, gardening, and botany exams during a 23-month training course. Family, I want to introduce you to our first graduating class!" The crowd erupted again!

The surprise would give hundreds of business owners a venue to produce their products, work with their target market, all while making great money. Not to mention, national and global distributors. With this, MLK Drive nor the Union will never be the same again, and it was for the better. Now, with the Greek Coalition in alliance, we added thousands of educated and highly resourceful women and men to the growing movement!

These had been some trying times for the people. This celebration and earned reward was a token for our great community accomplishments. We started so much on a dream, but now it has turned into a collective thought, mission, that propelled us into the next era of peace and excellence here in the city. We the people had so much to celebrate! People of all backgrounds from all over the state came to kick it with us. It was all love.

Everyone was having fun, while laughter and great vibes still circulated the room. Selah and Xho wrapped up the event. Gone half the night, Za and I finally caught up with Azzi and Zina.

"Where my chips and water at tho?" Zina asked before we even reached them.

"Girl, y'all ass been gone the whole night, I been ate those chips. We can get something when we leave if you want," I replied.

"Nah nevermind, I'ma ride with DJ and Azzi back home," Zina stated then looking down at her phone.

"Ok cool, where is DJ anyway? Y'all left dude all alone," I said, wondering.

"He's not with y'all?" Azzi said frantically.

"Uh no, was he supposed to be?" I replied, mildly chuckling.

"I thought y'all were going to be over there with him?" Azzi said as she continued looking around in frustration.

"Shaking my head at you, Syr. First, you ate my chips now you losing whole ass boyfriends," Zina said jokingly.

"First off, those chips were hella fire and I'm happy I ate them," I replied quickly. Everyone stood there, looking at me.

"Secondly??" Zina asked.

"Oh, that's it, those chips were fire," I answered.

Everyone stood there, looking at me with a blank stare. Realizing how mad they were, I replied, "Ohh, so y'all legit mad about this nigga being missing in here? Maybe he's somewhere with the single folks. Since that's what he looked like all night playing Fornite on his phone after y'all ditched him!"

"No really?!" Azzi asked, concerned.

"Don't listen to that fool, we went exploring after y'all left," Za said to ease Azzi's stress. Azzi ignored her comment then turned to look for DJ.

Before she could travel 10 feet, we heard someone yell Azzi's name. We all turned to see DJ walking up to Azzi with 2 dozen white Roses.

"Ok DJ, I see you!" I overheard Zina say to herself.

Getting closer and closer, we watched as DJ approached Azzi. I looked at Za, then at Zina, then thought to myself, "Fuck, is this nigga bout to propose or some shit?"

I snapped out of my pondering to hear Zina say, "Bish, I mean most eloquent African Queen, those flowers are for you! You better hug that man!"

I looked at Azzi smile as her eyes began to water. He walked to her and handed her the flowers. Azzi smiled, leaned into his arms and gave him a kiss. Za and Zina made noises to cheer them on. Azzi cradled the flowers as if it was a baby of hers.

"Where my flowers cornball?!" Za pinch me and said.

"Ouch! Hell! What I tell you about that pinching mess. Only flowers I'm worried about right now are hemp and bud. They can keep everything else," I replied, serious as hell.

Zina walked over to us then said, "We're about to go home y'all. What are y'all about to be on?"

"Probably hang out a little longer then head in," Za replied. "Hold up! Where's Selah? Is he still here?" I asked, looking around.

"We just saw him before we saw you. He said he'll catch up with us tomorrow at the event wrap up meeting. He had to head to an emergency meeting tonight. Xho's team has everything covered," Zina said, walking away.

"Bet, well, we out this piece too then. Let's shake," I said eagerly to Za. Everyone was leaving, so we did the same.

Top where you are, top where you can see above the trees.

Clouds of accomplishments keep you high and away.

Dodging mountains and eagles, the feeling of power is regal.

Look at him soar and it's all legal.

Go. Go tell the people I see you, above me, you're who I'm trying to reach and bleach the nonsense to teach the conscious.

Do you want to fly boy?

Do you want to fly girl?

Then fly! Fly with me higher!

Vibrate higher in the sky as we accomplish the dreams many are scared to chase to conquer to live in their happiness.

Where's your base, your roots, the bricks that built your launch pad child?

Your power and purpose find it and fly with the Gods that created you, yes, you at the top atop tops of your peaks.

Love is what you seek, prosperity is what you'll meet.

Ring! Ring! Ring! I jumped up with my phone on my chest and Za laying next to me. I looked at the time and realized I dosed off at Za's house. "Fuck! It's 330am!" I said, grabbing the phone to answer it. Hoping it wasn't my uncle, I flipped it over and saw it was Azzi, I quickly answered. Immediately I heard her yelling into the phone!

"They killed Selah! He's gone!" she screamed into the phone.

"Hold up what, they killed Selah?" I said, waking up Za.

"Two off duty police officers pulled him over and shot him. He killed one and got away, but hey found his truck burning on the eastside! His body was found in it! They said he reached, so they opened fire!" she said, crying hysterically.

"Fuck! Where y'all at now?!" I yelled curiously into the phone.

"We just left the crime scene," she replied.

"I'll meet y'all at your crib!" I finished then hung up.

Za kept asking me what was going on as I frantically put my clothes back on. I replied, "The fuckin cops killed Selah. Put your clothes on. I need you to take me to their crib!"

Heading to the house, silence struck the entire ride. Our thoughts wondered in the possible truths, lies, and outcomes of tonight's events. When we got to the house, cars were lined up around the block. A night that started so well, now covered the city in a depressing regressive fog.

As we entered the house, we were greeted by team and other community members. When Azzi spotted me, she ran and embraced me. Holding me tight I could feel her chest beating against my stomach. Zina joined in. "Everything is going to be ok, y'all! Your father equipped all of us with what it takes to continue his legacy and progress, not only ourselves but our people as well!" I held them, stating as the crowd of close friends and family looked on.

Days passed and funeral arrangements of the great community leader, man, and entrepreneur, Selah, were made. The funeral line stretched across the city. Selah's funeral brought the entire city together for the ceremony. Generals from every hood, politicians, famous folks, and so many more all spoke on his behalf, revealing their loyalty and friendship. The tears from the city could've replaced the Mississippi. We all mourned as we buried the burned mangled body found in the torched truck, Selah. Strangers and once enemies consoled each other, friends and family embraced one another, all remembering his message of unity, prosperity, and peace. Many vowed to turn the city into the vision Selah dreamt of that day. His death brought the city together in ways nothing else could. After the funeral, people stayed together and motivated. Strapped with a mission, the people began to put in work.

With the grand opening of Cokelys, black-owned restaurants were popping up all around the city. Black-owned Asian and Chinese Food restaurants. Black-owned pizzerias, and Mexican spots. The food was delicious and the restaurants were one of a kind. Cokelys caused businesses that funneled millions from the community to close down and never return. In addition, more and more people where investing and cultivating the crop on their own land successfully. With demands for our hemp gear and products, we were forced to purchase more land and bulk up on orders from our distributors. That became a hassle. So finally, we ended up just opening a shop with team members, volunteers, and some paid employees. They wove, then printed and shipped off the merchandise to boutiques around the city, helping to keep product on shelves. With so much land invested by the people of the city, we were getting close to having enough to now produce hemp oil. Which if we could stabilize the oil with current motors, it could replace tradition oil. If we could create a community industry that went nationwide? Worldwide? It would be a sure way to create a stable future for the people of St. Louis, and possibly, abroad.

Time seemed to speed up after Selah's funeral, the team of Xhosah, PPC and Selah made so many strides quick.

People had calmed, and the buzz of Selah's death had come to a cease. Though the things built from it were booming, bringing the city much success. Ties were built with people from all over and nonbelievers in the cause were converted. The city had a pulse of progression and purpose. I took it as a blessing to be a part of producing that feeling, we all did.

One day, leaving a meeting with the North and South Side Coalition about the upcoming School Parade Wars. The parade was an epic citywide festival with a purpose of gold. It was to showcase the talents each educational institution around the city had to offer. "Man, this year's parade will be one for the books!" I thought to myself as I walked down the streets of the Westside, leaving the library.

Coming across the Hodiamont tracks, I saw a seemingly homeless man on a bike at the top of the alley just staring at me. Today, the tracks were almost empty of barters and goods markets. I took a glimpse but paid it no mind and kept walking to the house. Still walking, I reached for my phone to check for the time. I dug in my pocket, nope. Another pocket, then another. "Nope! Nope! Fuck! Where is my phone?!" I uttered to myself in frustration. Maybe I left it at the library, I thought. I turned to head back, that's when I saw the homeless man now standing at the edge of the alley on his bike. I paid it no mind and headed back to the library. Before I could take 10 steps, the man held something up. I slowed down and looked closer. It was my fucking phone! Trying to play it off, I said, "Thanks Family, that's my phone, I was worried I lost it!"

The homeless man stood firm and said, "You did lose it, lil scrub ass nigga!" And took off up the alley on his bike.

"The fuck fam! Aye nigga whatchu on! Gimme my shit!" I said, taking off, chasing after the bike up the alley. The man was too big for the bike, so he wasn't going that fast. But before I could gain any real ground, he turned into a yard of a vacant school. One of the few that still exist in St. Louis.

When I got to the fence of the school, I saw the homeless man running into the building through some random hole in the wall. Knowing this wasn't the best decision, I followed anyway. I needed my phone. If this old ass clown finds a way to unlock my shit, he's going to have access to…nevermind, that doesn't matter. I ran into the hole in the wall after him. I pulled my .38 out my book bag. I've been carrying it since the funeral and was ready to use it, just in case buddy was past talking. Creeping through the building, dodging debris and piles of old school desk. That's when I heard some music playing up the stairs. I stopped to get a clear listen. Then uttered to myself, "Fuck is that Beyonce? I got caught lackin by a bum that listens to Beyonce?!" I cocked my weapon and headed up the steps. I followed the music, hoping it led me to this fool that just tried to Debo me for my phone. The music was getting louder, I was getting closer. I walked upon a door, that's when I heard footsteps. I peeped around the corner to see a figure dancing. I took a deep breath and barged into the room, only to see Selah dressed as a homeless man, sitting on a couch, trying to break into my phone.

He looked up and said, "Oh, what's good family, what took you so long?"

Confused and shocked, I said, "Hold up, what the fuck?!'

I looked over as the hooded dancing figure said, "Syr, bro chill."

Shocked and bewildered of what was going on, I asked, "Azzi, is that you?"

"Yes boy!" she said, taking off the hood.

"Well surprise," Selah stood and said, throwing me my phone. I stood there in shock of what I was seeing. He took off all of his bummy shirts and revealed multiple shot wounds wrapped in now bloody bandages. "Next time, I'll wear a vest," he said jokingly as he noticed me staring.

In a daze, staring at the man I looked up to for almost all my life, alive in the flesh after we buried him. "Jesus, this nigga is Jesus," I said to myself, still trying to wrap my mind around what was happening. I walked up to him and gave him a long hug and welcomed him back. I sat down and grabbed my water out my bag and said, "Family, what happened, I thought they killed you?"

"Don't worry. Just know it's good to have friends on both sides," Selah replied with a wink.

He always had a plan, a way, he was always 5 steps ahead of everyone. Sitting down, pondering his next master plan, I asked, "So what's next, I know you have some more slick shit up your sleeve?"

He laughed and said, "I do but first, look who I found," Selah said, pointing into a room. I walked in slowly and saw a figure putting a chain on in the mirror. It was my brother, Kano.

I ran over to him and gave him a hug then said, "My nigga, you're out! Show me some love!"

Kano looked at me smiling and said, "I haven't been far, but I'm finally out. So much has changed. A chance to renew myself and my purpose, the future is ours for the taking. Nothing will ever be the same now, lil bro."

Now that we knew Selah was alive and working with my newly released brother, Kano, a feeling of ease and hope filled our mission. Life went on as if they weren't around although we could see the progress in the community changing. We were ordered to stay low and under the radar for a while until things cooled down. We as a team met often to update Selah and work on new community projects.

After Selah's faked death, Azzi and DJ grew apart and decided to end their relationship. Zina's parents were fearful of the aftermath of Selah's death, so they made her cutback on hanging with us, and forced her to work at the family Herb & Med Shoppe. Though we didn't see Zina as much anymore, we all stayed close.

Our mission never changed. Always busy on projects, you couldn't really tell if Azzi was bothered by everything going on. We were always working. Working for the people and for the future. It was our deepest passion to see our people prosperous with a peace of mind. With me always in the community or with the team, Za and I began to spend less and less time together. With conflicting schedules and goals, we always seemed to be on different waves. Eventually, all our conversations centered on how we can make more money. Like it was a race to richest. I got tired of running, my true race was to empower the people. Soon, like two trains passing in the night, we parted ways, but remained fuck buddies and business partners. Eventually, our lil sex sessions ceased when she moved to Mississippi to start a real estate and contracting business. Though we didn't talk often after she left, our cool vibes and friendship never skipped a beat when we did.

Free of our relationships, my friendship with Azzi began to grow back into its old luster. Often spending hours in the library working and studying to stay ahead of the game. This brings us to the beginning where we left off.

Aye you,

You walk with a rhythm of the earth,

made to surf the most daunting waves,

Infinite like the universe

no being can calculate or assimilate your worth,

for the darkness between the stars

is what holds the answers to your birth,

Aye...you,

Look at the way you move,

Feel that groove from the energy you spew, natural mechanics so smooth.

The universe chose you to absorb the life it spew,

Definition of extraterrestrial because you embody all,

you extra extra special,

celestial original vessel you,

Embrace your timelessness divine'ness

Only suns out shine this heavenly fine'ness

Blindless foes attempts to devalue and ignore your glows and grows

Forget your woes, for the universe has already chose

You were first and you will be last

You were first and you'll be last,

getting you, yea you, to take your rightful spot,

is the task...

OUT OF DODGE

(Back to Life. Back to Reality. Then beginning where the escape left off)

Slicing through the dark back streets of the Westside, bumping 'Picturing Me Rolling', I turned to the backseat and suggested, "Let's go over Shareef's house, nobody would suspect for us to go over there. We can leave in the morning."

"You sure?!" Azzi said, questioning the idea.

"Shit, why not? We need to hurry up and get out these streets, plus his house is the closest from where we are," Zina proclaimed.

"Well, hit him up and let's see," Azzi folded and suggested.

"Nah, actually, we're just going to pop up. Turn your phones off or they'll find us before we even get there," Kano said calmly but sternly. He then reached for the volume dial and turned the tunes up.

I looked at Azzi then turned around and said, "Well, it's a right up here at the light," I said, pointing ahead.

"I know where he stays, just sit back," Kano confessed.

The car went silent before Azzi broke it, saying, "How the hell you know where Reef stay, creep?"

Kano cut down the radio. Staring in the rearview mirror at Azzi, he said, "Same way I know where all your fuckin friends and family stay. It's my job. You think you can just be the daughter of one of the most powerful black men in the Midwest and not be a target? Think about where the fuck we live, you think y'all cute young asses can just try and change the nation and these folks just gone let y'all? All your asses have been saved more than once and you don't even know it. Thank your father for that."

"So bro, yo ass been following us?" I asked for clarity.

Kano just looked at me then turned up the music. As he hit the corner and stepped on the gas, I could hear Zina mumble, "The sweet bliss of ignorance. I guess."

We pulled up to the ducked off block in Baden where Reef stayed. The lights were on. "It looks like he's home. I'll go knock on the door," I said as Kano parked the car under a tree. I jumped out of the car and ran up the steps to the door. I opened the screen door and knocked softly. Before I could finish, the door swung open wide.

"Nigga, why you knocking like I don't own this mafucka. What you running from somebody or some shit?" Reef stood in the door way, inquiring with a smile.

"The fuck, were you standing next to the door!? Nevermind, yes family! Azzi, Zina, and my bro, Kano, parked under the tree, we need to duck off for the night," I briefly explained.

Reef quickly replied, "Say less bro. Tell them to pull around and park under the tree in the backyard. They can take the tarp off the Impala and cover the whip up."

"Bet!" I replied and ran back to the car. We drove around back and did just that.

When we got into the house, I introduced Reef to Kano. "I appreciate the hospitality brother," Kano said, having a seat on the couch.

"Yea, you not even knowing how clutch you are right now," Zina said, heading toward the kitchen. Azzi followed.

"So what else can I do to help? Want me to roll up?" Reef said.

"Yea, let's have a session to brainstorm," I replied.

Azzi and Zina walked back in right on time with plates of food as Reef finished rolling. "You gotta let me get some of that, Azzi! You know you love me! I'm hungry just like you!" I pleaded, scooting closer to her and her plate of delectable pastries.

"Here, don't eat all my stuff, lil boy!" she replied, rolling her eyes then watching me like a hawk as I grabbed a cannoli.

"Aye, let's check the news real quick to see if they're saying anything about what happened today," Zina suggested, taking a break from her breaded snack.

"Ugh the news! Just for a second, that mess is toxic!" Shareef said, hitting the power button to the flat screen tv.

"But sometimes informative, nonetheless," Azzi added.

Reef changed the channel to the local news and it didn't take long before our story slid across the screen. "Breaking News; 3 cops kidnapped and missing by local Activist and family! None have been found!"

Reef paused, then turned around slowly and looked at us then uttered, "Bruh what the fuck y'all been on all day? Y'all got like 4 stars, and it look like it's 'bout to be 5 in a minute! Y'all need a plan to get the fuck out of dodge family. Not that ol' hide on the Westside Selah shit, no offense Azzi, but I'm talking shaking spot completely. Like be gone forever."

"But they didn't have any pictures of us," Azzi said, looking for a sign of hope.

"By tomorrow, they will. They gone have all y'all ugly asses posted on the screen. So, you better think of something fast," Kano said, still sitting in the corner.

"Hold up, you're with us, they're looking for you too," Zina said.

"For now, I am. I have a plan, I always have. I advise you to get one of your own," Kano responded in a cold tone.

"Damn, this nigga turned mean fast, clearly I was mistaken. You can keep that vibe that way," Zina replied, sitting back in her chair. Kano just stared at her.

"Anyway, y'all, we need to think. If this could be our last night here in the city, how can we go out with a bang? Something that the people will remember forever," Azzi said, refocusing us all.

We all sat in silence for a few minutes before Reef said, "Smoke on it?"

"Let's!" I said, leaning up on the couch, hoping to calm my flustered nerves.

"Agreed," Azzi said, confirming the thought as well.

"I guess I'll indulge," Zina said, joining in.

Sitting in the corner, observing our every move like a hawk on prey, Kano chimed in, "With all that happened today, answer me this. Y'all really think this is the best time to be smoking and eating pastries in shit?"

We all looked at each other, then Azzi replied, "Actually, after everything that happened today, I think this is the perfect time for a blunt and pastries. We're gonna be here the night, big bro, let's chill and think of our next move."

Kano sat back in his chair slowly and said, "You right."

As the first blunt went in orbit and the pastries filled our stomachs, we brainstormed on our next move.

"We should start a "dress like them" prank. Have a bunch of people your complexion with fros and dreads to put make up on to make them look exactly like you. That'll fuck em up y'all! It's hella people your color with locs," Reef suggested seriously.

"It'll be even crazier if we got them all to take pics as you under your Bookface profile," Zina added.

"Yea, that would confuse a lot of people for sure, but that'll hide you. How will we keep the movement going? That's what Selah would want, that's what we need to figure out," Kano said, refocusing the discussion.

"How about we just tell them about our 5-year campaign and some of the future projects to help out, not only our city, but cities like St. Louis as well? We can give the black community around the country the blueprint," I suggested. It was all we had. If the people bought in, it would be all we needed. Joining cities and cultures alike for the cause of prosperity and peace of mind. The 5-year collective economics campaign would put us ahead for many decades to come. Filled with youthful hope, we began filming the videos that could change the paradigm of black existence in America.

We concluded to record videos telling them the blueprint and plans explaining how just uniting beyond race or color, but on morals and ideas could change the tides of peace of mind in the direction of the people. We can start by telling them we're innocent, then tell them how they too can join the People's Union. If cities alike join us, we can create industries up and down the Mississippi. Like if St. Louis makes clothes, then Memphis can make bricks, paper and installation, maybe Detroit can make oils and medicines. We gave many suggestions.

We mentioned the restructuring of the education system. A rotating People's casino that traveled from city to city like a circus. All the money raised will be put back into the community that earned it. Not to 1 or 2 greedy negros. We also suggested black lotteries where portions are put back into the community. After all, billions were spent on lottery tickets with few to no community winners. It was time the people had control of such a mass amount of funds.

We explained to them the benefits of the Even Field Sports Plan. Like the Trades plan, all kids are introduced to all major sports options from grade school through high school. This allowed the youth of the movement to flood all sports arenas and dominate. From hockey, Lacrosse, to gymnastics, golf, MMA, ice skating and more. The Olympic and all-star teams were beginning to darken up quickly. Along with many professionals coming back and teaching younger generations, this ultimately gave every child access to potential lucrative sport activities. Creating more and putting everything in full circle. Seeing as for decades, millions of boys and girls devoted their time and energy into mainstream sports only to fail and join a dying economy. With our programs, we vowed to make every sport mainstream, and have it dominated by the People. We also explained the benefit of getting athletes, public figures alike to sponsor and support the 5-year campaign publicly and privately. The more the people buy in, the better. The community and people will reap the benefits of the businesses and its earnings. With this blueprint, we knew in no time, our videos would go viral.

"Now that we've found a way to get the message out, we need to find a way to get out of the country," I announced, still not sure of what that meant. Where would we go? Where would we stay? How long will our money last? Are we going to have to be on some Bear Grills type shit? Will we ever be able to come home? I thought.

"Out the country and on the run? Hell, am I Carmen Sandiego now? I guess," Azzi looked up and said.

"You gone damn near have to be if they find out what happened tonight," Kano added, being the opposite of reassuring.

"I have an idea! We need to hit the store to get some burn out phones," Kano suggested. "What if they see us on camera? Reef, you think you can go? Nobody is looking for you," Zina added. "True, but I have a better idea. I'll be right back," Reef replied. "Nigga, where you going?" I asked as he began to head to the door after grabbing his keys. "I'm going to get the phones, I'll be right back," Reef said, leaving the house.

We sat, patiently waiting Reef's return. Only a short period of time had passed when the screen door opened, and the door unlocked. Reef walked in with bags in his hands. "Damn bro where you go, you get the phones?" I asked. He handed me the bag of phones without saying a word, only pointing to the phone as if it was an important call. We dumped the bag of phones on the couch and began to look through them. "You sure these are throwaways, look like somebody had these things up their ass since the 90's," I said, noticing the sketchy condition of the devices.

Finally getting off of the phone, Reef said, "Chill, that was one of my lil honey dips, I had to reschedule the plans for her to come through and teach me some anatomy."

"Perv," Azzi said.

"Call me what you like but you know the creator created a beautiful being when he dreamt of the black woman," Reef replied.

Azzi looked Reef in the eyes with her lips turned up as he smirked then said, "You eat booty, don't you?"

Looking her right back in her eyes, he replied, "You damn right. I'm grown!"

"Aye errbody, shut the fuck up right now! What we not about to do is talk about eating no butt!" Kano yelled, silencing everybody.

A few moments later, I broke it by changing the subject and asking Reef, "So where you get these phones from bro?"

"To be honest, I got them from some hoes on Broadway," Reef responded, rolling another blunt.

"Hoes on Broadway? You mean like slanging ass type hoes?" I asked for clarity.

Reef looked up as if to be thinking then said, "I mean if you want to describe them in that light, yes. They get paid to pleasure people, strangers mostly. But shit, most hoes giving it up for free so who can hate? If I was a hoe like slanging ass hoe, I would prefer to be called a pleasure professional. Sounds classier."

Azzi and Zina dropped the phones and instantly went to the bathroom. "Plus, they gave me their phones for a $150, I can't talk shit now. And whose gonna want to track all these hoes phones anyway?" Reef continued.

"Bro, how you know so many hoes?" I asked out of curiosity.

Reef shrugged his shoulders then said, "Man, my uncle's a pimp and been a pimp since the early 2000's. Told me, pinky ring it, until you get the wedding ring."

"Man, I thought pimping died. A long time ago. All the black women seem so smart and righteous, these days, like selling ass would be the last thing on their mind. Maybe I've been away too long," Kano said, scratching his head, still chilling in the corner.

"Oh, ain't none of them Black. And believe me, pimping will live as long as money, drugs, pussy, and women with low self-esteem are around," Reef said, firing up and putting another blunt in orbit. The ladies came back in and cleaned the phones with disinfectant wipes. Hella times. Now that we had the phones and a plan, it was time to execute.

Own our addictions, our flaws, our flaws are our addictions

plain sight encryptions of loves detention and unworthy repentance tons
of times, while embracing the crimes with primal minds.

Shines of darkness block the signs.

It's time we own our addictions, our flaws, squares pills, herbs and
alcohols aid the falls of Temple walls.

But not by the hands of we, profits go to the hands of sheep that escape
our streets.

A King mustn't flee into sleep for we are the chosen, just frozen.

We must learn to grow and poe our own poison, so when it's all said
and done, we can say it was our flaws, our addictions that we owned
and condoned.

After some scripting, filming, and editing, the videos were ready to be sent to Xhosah to send and spread through famous circles. With no time for change, we could only hope they saw our vision and acted. We set it up to release the videos to the public strategically to gain a bigger buzz but to also throw the boys off our trail. We stayed up all night, planning a seemingly perfect get-away. With no rest and a pieced together plan, we decided to have Reef drive us to Memphis to get on the greyhound. It was a precaution just in case cops were covering stations in St. Louis. Once we got there, we would part ways with Reef.

With the morning sun only a few hours away, we packed up some essentials and loaded up for the road. "I wish we had more time to plan, everything fills rushed," I said, going over every possibility in my head.

"Actually, y'all should've been gone! I don't even know why I'm here waiting to be locked away forever with a group of kids," Kano said, standing back in calm but serious voice.

"I'm glad we don't have to listen to yo Negative Nancy ass no more after tonight," Azzi said, climbing into the backseat.

"Come on, Zina!" I said, holding the seat up for her.

She looked down and said, "I'm not going, I can't go, my everything is here. My family, I won't leave them to run from these bastards. I can't. If they want me, they gotta come to the hood to get me." Azzi jumped out of the car in tears and ran to Zina.

"What do you mean?! You can't stay, what if…" Azzi said before Zina cut her off sternly, saying with tears in her eyes, "I said what I said, Azzi. Now go!" Face red and swollen from the feelings attached to departing a kindred soul, Azzi hugged her tightly, said her goodbyes, then got into the car. I followed with my parting goodbyes then jumped into the car as well. We hit a few corners then crossed the bridge into Illinois, and like that, we were gone.

Flying down the highway tailing a rabbit we caught a few towns back, we sat silently listening to the tunes of Thelonius Monk and Cultrain. "Y'all, I have an idea," Azzi said from the backseat. I cut down the radio, so Reef and I could listen closely. "When I was growing up, Pops and I used to come to Memphis to see friends of the family. I think I remember where they stay. Maybe we can get some help from them," she suggested, looking for ways to better our situation.

"Shit, I'm down. We need as much help as we can get now. Call them to see what's up," I replied, looking out the window at the miles of farms that lined the horizon.

"We can't use our phones, plus, I don't have their number anymore. I was little last time I saw them. Never thought I'll need for some crazy shit like this," Azzi said, rubbing her head in deeper frustration.

"Hold up, so y'all just tryna pop up over some nigga house you ain't seen or talk to in yeeeeaaarrs! How you know they still stay where you think that stay? What if he doesn't remember yo ass, or worse, he turned into the boys!? I don't know family, I'm not a fan of just popping up on niggas," Reef said, not feeling comfortable with Azzi's suggestion.

"Man, we popped up over yo crib and you helped us. Bro what choice do we have?" I stated.

"That's because I know y'all goofy ass but ok, I'll ride. Just tell me where to go when we get close to the city," Reef replied as he stepped on the gas and turned up the classic tunes.

When we got to Memphis, Azzi guided through the back streets until we came to a dark block. "I think this is the street," Azzi whispered.

We rolled down the street slowly until Azzi saw a familiar property. When we pulled up to the house, it was pitch dark in every direction. "You sure this is it?" I asked for reassurance.

Azzi looked out the window to take another look. "This ain't the time for yo ass to be guessing, Azzi," Reef said nervously, sitting in the car, staring at the dark house, seemingly empty.

"Yes, this is it, I remember playing right over there with his family hecky years back," Azzi replied confidently.

"Years back?! You sure this nigga ain't dead or moved away?" Reef said, becoming more nervous. He was starting to make me nervous too. That's when a flash came from the porch.

"What the fuck was that?! Y'all see that flash?!" I said as we all stared at the house.

"Yes fool! We looking too! What y'all think it is?" Reef said.

"It's him! I'm getting out," Azzi said, pushing my seat, trying to open the door.

That's when we heard a deep voice, "Stay in the car." I hurried and closed the door, as a dark figure moved from behind a nearby tree.

"The fuck? Should I pull off? Cause this is usually the time when a scary movie starts, or a smart black person pulls the fuck off!" Reef said frantically. The figure moved closer out of the darkest and mist toward the car. Getting closer, Reef suddenly hit his headlights.

"No chill! Wait, I think that's him! Azoo! Azoo Akaru! Is that you?" Azzi said softly out the window.

Coming into sight, he came to the window and said, "Indeed, young Princess. I'm already aware of the situation, time is of the essence so listen closely! You too, Syr. Take these bags and utilize everything in them to get to the Strait of Gibraltar as soon as possible. Someone will be waiting for you. You're needed in Africa!"

Goosebumps covered my body. My mind was bombarded with questions and curiosity, but I sat back and stayed silent to see Azzi's response. Seemingly confused, she looked him close in the face and then calmly said, "What? How the fuu...." He briefly cut her off saying, "Follow the directions to the bus station, make your way to Florida and board the cruise ship. I.Ds, passports, tickets are all in the bag. Use what you need to make it home to the Ndio Umoja! GO Now!" Reef stepped on the gas and floored it down the street.

"Azzi what the fuck is he talking about? Home? The Ndudu what? What's going on?" I turned around, asking Azzi.

"I don't know! I'm just hearing this shit just like you!" she replied.

"Nigga slow down, you don't even know where we going!" I yelled to Reef, holding on to the door.

"Yea, I do! The hell away from here!" Reef said, flying down the street then turning wildly down an alley.

"Everyone calm down please!" Azzi pleaded loudly. Reef slowed the car down as everyone came to a calm.

"Man, the nigga just made it seem like somebody was chasing us in shit, but my bad," Reef said, breaking the brief moment of silence.

"I mean, they kind of still is, but that doesn't mean drive like a maniac. So, chill. Syr, let's check our bags!" Azzi said, regaining order.

I opened my bag quickly. Undoing the straps, a digital map to the bus station fell unto my lap. "Reef, here's the map, cut it on and let's catch this bus out of here," I said still digging through the mysterious bag. Next, I pulled out a wallet. I opened it immediately only to be blown back by my eyes. "How they get a picture of me? I don't even remember taking this!" I said, pulling out an ID with a strange name and a picture of myself.

"I have one too, and my picture cute," Azzi replied.

"Here, let me see what you have in yours," I said, reaching for Azzi's bag to curiously search through it for clues. She closed it quickly and pulled it out of reach and stated.

"No, there are personal things in here. There should be some in yours." I slowly turned around and continued to search through mine for any clue I could find.

We came up with a plan to pass our personal phones from friend to friend, waiting a few days then having them call a number and send a coded message to one of many cell phones we mailed across the country. Before we left, we gave our phones to Kano and told him to begin the process. Even this apparent complex plan would only buy us so much time. We needed to hurry.

Finally arriving to the bus station, Azzi quickly said her goodbyes to Reef and jumped out of the car to catch the already waiting bus. I grabbed my bags and hugged Reef goodbye. He's a friend I considered to be a brother. "Until next family!" I said, giving him one last dap.

"You already know bro, keep yo head up! Aye and if you can, bring back some of that African Kush for the next study!" Reef replied, laughing and getting into the car.

I laughed then threw up the fist. I didn't know what was next for us, or if we were ever going to get a chance to see our home, or a familiar face again. As unfortunate as it was, we had to focus. We had to escape the US.

I ran to catch the bus, and surprisingly boarded with ease. Already on the bus, I joined Azzi in the back. "Well, that was easy," I whispered to Azzi as I sat down.

"Yea, but the real challenge is keeping it easy, at least until we get to Africa," she replied.

"Facts, let's just chill and think about what's going on, and how we're going to get there," I said, attempting to relax our minds on the 20-hour ride south. More than likely, I did the opposite. The ride was long, long as fuck but we thought it would be the safest way to Miami.

Crammed into the tight seats, surrounded by strangers with questionable hygiene, it was a task to get comfortable. Sleeping for me wouldn't be an option on this journey. But not for Azzi. She rested peacefully on my shoulder whenever she became bored with reading and games of tic-tac-toe. When I wasn't watching the terrain change out window or sketchy bus riders, I watched her sleep. Even unconscious, she glowed with life, beauty, and purpose. Each deep breath of peace that filled her body, brought tranquility to my soul. Though running for our lives and freedom, I cherished every moment I could share the same space with her. The bus was quiet and dark most of the way through the South. Guarding Azzi and our bags with my life, I never left her side the entire ride. By next afternoon, we had arrived in Miami. We jumped off the bus and immediately headed for the port of Miami to catch the ship. We were pressed for time. So, we hurled a cab and made our way to the port.

"Azzi family, I have a feeling this is going to be a lot harder than getting into the bus station," I said as we walked up to the huge Port of Miami.

"Naturally, but how do we even get in?" Azzi asked, surveying the structure.

"Look, there's a line over there, let's go," I said, pointing to a section of the building in the distance.

"Ok, pull out your ticket and passport," Azzi said, grabbing her bag.

We headed to the line of vacationers and tried our best to blend in and go unnoticed. I was nervous, and I could tell Azzi was too. We stood in line, patiently waiting with our IDs, passports, and tickets, that were all fake. My palms began to sweat as I clutched my items firmly. Entering the building, we could see cops with dogs the size of loveseats roaming freely. The creatures were sniffing the asses and luggage of everyone in its path.

"Syr, I hope this works," Azzi uttered softly, grabbing my hand and locking her fingers with mine. I embraced her touch. I wanted to relieve her of her worry and fear. Though deep down, I knew this could be our last chance, I reassured her we will be ok.

When it was our turn, we calmly walked up and handed the attendant our information. After scanning the documents and examining every curve and feature on our face, one by one, we were let through to the metal detectors. Not having any weapons on us, we passed through easily. Then out of nowhere, one of the monstrous dogs began to bark furiously. The cop ran over to me with the angry alerted animal.

"Sir, please stand still!" the cop yelled. I froze in my tracks. "Do you have anything on you?" the cop asked, patting me down.

"No, I do not," I responded.

"Where you going?" he continued as the dog barked, looking into my eyes. "I'm going on a cruise of the Atlantic with my wife," I said, smiling and allowing the officer to search me. He looked up and then grabbed my ID. Studying the information to see any fault, he finally looked up and said, "You can go." The dog calmed down and they left. As the officer and his pet walked away, I hurried and grabbed my bag then we headed to the ship.

Walking away briskly, Azzi turned to me smiling then said, "Your wife? I'm your wife now, Syr?"

I looked at her and grinned. "Azzi, you can be whatever you like if we make it to our destination safely."

She smiled then laughed. We spotted our ship, then headed straight to it.

Once aboard the cruise ship, we walked around momentarily, sightseeing the eloquent ship, until we finally made it to our secluded room. Once I opened up the door, Azzi ran in and flopped on the bed then kicked off her shoes. I decided to join her. "Safe! We made it to a bed! Now it's time to find some food! After this nap," she said with her face buried in the plush pillows. After a brief moment of silence, just like that, we fell into a deep slumber.

Breathes deep like the black sea, move me gracefully into calm sub realities.

Those of bliss, peace of mind for my mind.

I go deeper into purpose.

Abnormal thoughts of service to create functional systems of peace, peace I seek, peace of mind for my kind.

I weep, no more herd of sheep I heard, only lions, elephants, gorillas run these jungle streets of concrete.

Now. Peace of mine in every vine.

Love drowning the mind with hope threating her like a shrine, now peace of mind for all kind.

We woke well rested, but with stomachs filled with air. Leaving out of the corner cabin, we headed in search of food. Wondering through the many hallways, we stumbled upon a casino. The cozy seats were filled with old men and women cradling buckets of coins ready for a day of sacrifice. We walked through briskly to be sure to go unnoticed. Finally making it to the deck, we spotted a group of people walking with plates of food. We eagerly walked to the room where the group came from. Feeling our stomachs touching our back, we hit the corner and there it was. A glamorous spread of fruits and pastries, veggies and more! My mouth filled with water, before I could say a word, Azzi pushed me out of the way and grabbed a plate. I followed. Walking the chow line, we filled our plates with various pastries and fruits until our plates could hold no more. Spotting some seats on deck where we could eat our meal, we headed toward the door. Passing the many skeet short patrons, we opened the door and entered the radiant blue ora of the ocean. The glare of Amun (the Egyptian Sun God) danced vibrantly off the ocean's surface, sprinkling like a silent firework show. Its beauty stopped us in our tracks, the music of the crashing waves instantly hypnotizing us.

"Wow, I have never seen such a gorgeous sight. You see this Azzi!" I said, grabbing her hand and leading her to the edge of the deck.

"Boy, slow down before you make me waste my food!" Azzi yelled, following along, holding her plate of goods carefully. Maneuvering through the maze of beach chairs, we eagerly made our way. We posted as close to the edge as possible to get the best view of nature's majestic painting of the day's horizon.

"Syr, you think this is nice, wait until we get to Africa. It's truly the continent of Eden. A living and thriving paradise. You're going to be surrounded by beauty, just wait. Hold up, you know where we're going?" Azzi informed me and asked.

"Nope," I replied.

"I'm just saying the continent is beautiful, from what I remember as a child," she added for clarity.

Sitting out, we overheard a couple speaking of viral videos released by fugitives and how the people were buying into the message. "If this works, the US will never be the same," one said as we eavesdropped. "Well, that's a good thing, at least for the blacks. They're finally taking responsibility for the future of their people. Maybe our taxes will be lower now," the other responded, slightly laughing in amusement. The looks on their faces were ones of neutrality. We sat, unnoticed, listening to the thoughts of strangers. Hoping they understood, when from the looks it seemed they couldn't care less. Having enough, we headed back to our room to rest, and think of the new life that awaited.

Deep down, we knew the People watched because we made sense and we inspired. They watched because they saw us in them, they pictured the idea of freedom and peace of mind. It was tangible, and more than able to be accomplished. We hoped they got the message, loud and clear.

If you want to go fast, go alone, if you want to go far, go together…
so together, we went.

Azzi woke me up in the middle of the night, forcing my belongings into my arms. "It's time for us to go!" she quietly pleaded.

"What already? Nigga it feel like we're still in the middle of the ocean. Where the hell we going?" I replied, confused.

"Get your ass up and let's go before we miss our chance. We don't have time for questions!" she said sternly.

I immediately hopped up and got dressed. "Act casual," she said before leading into the hallway. We moved quickly and stealthily through the ship until we reached the deck.

"Now what? What are we doing my nigga? Nobody is after us all the way out here!" I asked, confused and trying to understand.

Azzi ran to the rail, then spotted a dim, blinking light on a small ship floating in the shadows of the night ocean. "There!" she said, grabbing me then pointing.

"So what? We suppose to help them on board or some shit?" I asked for clarity.

"We have to jump, idiot! This is our only shot!" Azzi yelled.

I turned to look around to see if somebody was coming. Nobody. Then I suddenly turned to look again, and there it was. A figure, walking out of the shadows into the light. It looked familiar, as it got closer, the moonlight revealed his face. It was the same man from the event the night Selah almost got killed. Recognizing him, I instantly told Azzi to jump! Seeing him coming, she leaped into the water. Getting closer, I took a deep breath then frog-splashed off the rail into the ocean where the mysterious ship awaited us.

Hitting the water like a rock, I frantically started fighting the monstrous waves and currents but to no avail. I thought to myself, *now this woman knew damn well I can't swim! I'm stupid because I followed her ass. Now I'm 'bout ta die!* I thought as I sank instantly into the deep dark obis. But before I could get my prayers out. Like a last wish, an arm reached into the water and grabbed me then helped me onboard. Coughing up water, cursing, and catching my breath, I looked up and saw 3 large dark figures standing firm in the darkness. I looked around and saw Azzi standing next to a slender figure draped in a black hooded robe. "Azzi, what's going on!?" I asked frantically.

"Syr, I have something to tell you. I haven't been completely honest with you this whole time," Azzi uttered with her head down before being cut off by the slender robed figure, "Spare him the worry, my Princess, it will only make him sea sick."

"Hol' up, what!?" I pleaded in pure confusion.

"Greetings young King! I am Assata, the Queen of the Ndio Umoji, and this is my daughter, Aaizza. I hope you are half the warrior they say you are, because it's going to be hell trying to sneak back into Africa!"

Wonder a world of Tours by Actors, Athletes, Artist.

they wouldn't even have to try they hardest.

Modest and honest are the talents that spew

…in you,

here and from a worldly view,

Gather thy littest melanated crew, to show who,

all that suffered indoctrination from schools and the medias view.

A slew of natural abilities amenities and cultural nobility,

culture culture vulture vulture can't bit the fleek.

So turn it around and use it against we?

Nah again,

WE will be the word that's heard across masses,

heels will hold asses…because of you.

Give us the stage and we'll show you what the people can do.

Enlighten illuminated minds that dwell in fuliginous spaces,

its due,

no longer chaperoned by the savage few that used lies to guide you.

We are here.

Short ropes made long by loved arms and legs

together we flock out of the dark hole of mud

and turn that bih to a whole ass tub

where we bask in prosperity and unified love for us.

Wash away our fears.

Scruba dub dub,

family, it's time for us to eat,

grub grub grub.

Oh, what joy when brothers dwell and swell in peace...

Art Gallery

Ready for you to Color

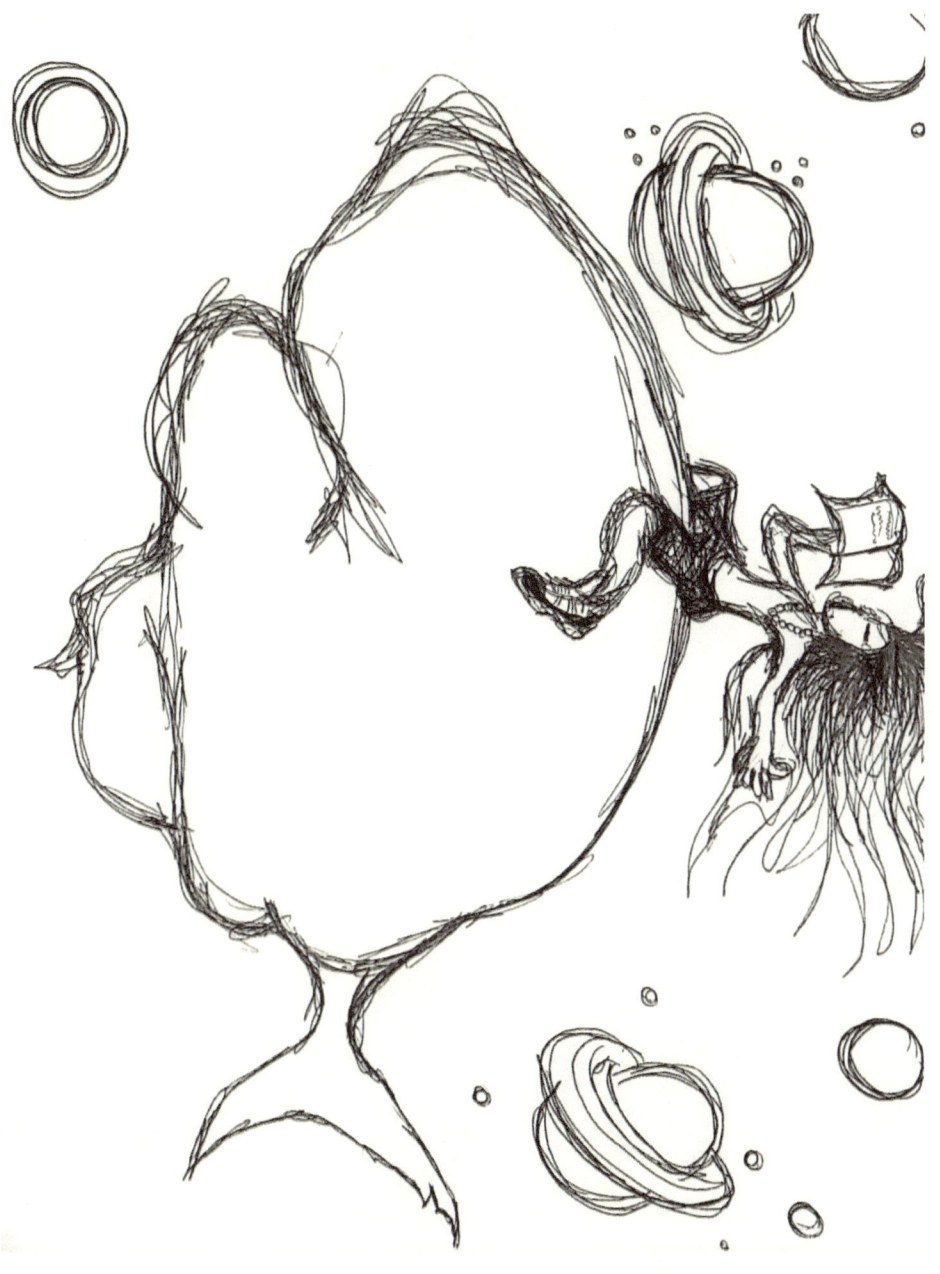

Diaries of the Founders

Syr Journal Entry #3

- National black tumbling, track & field, and martial art teams. Starting from kindergarten, so kids can master discipline/emotions.

- Families should be given professionally trained defense and attack dogs. ~~That can also flip~~

- Why they want to hold us back? Why they hate us when all we want is peace?

Zina Diary Entry #9

Ummm...

- ❖ *People should use toaster ovens instead of microwaves.*

- ❖ *Recycle baby clothes for first 10 years to humble all kids and save parents money.*

- ❖ *Strip mall on MLK with vintage used gear, threads sold by the union, and trusted union sponsors.*

- ❖ *Hemp gear doesn't produce microfibers which is toxic. (*don't forget to clean water filter)*

- ❖ *Women should stop using tampons. Shits toxic*

- ❖ *Stop using soft metals such as aluminum foil and plastics to* cook and store food.

❖ They still giving out free shots??? Shit will forever be sketchy. I'll pass....

❖ Would everyone being a germophobe help or hurt the population's immune system?

Kano Journal Entry #14

They got us fucked up

o Err nigga in prison or jail should go on strike from corporate labor until all facilities are proven to rehabilitate.

o Speed up court process. All inmates seen and judged within 3 days. No jail for traffic tickets, only community service. BMs and Ol' Birds/fathers visit often to make sure they're good during process to keep they ass focused on the goal.

Badgers Journal Entry #32

Random thoughts while on the run

Creation and things built from early African travel

through trial & error.

- For million years blacks lived and thrived in Africa learning every day rom trial and error, teaching the youth everything about the expanding world around them...They first learned and remembered through trial and error. Over centuries of proper execution and teaching it became common knowledge, even instinct. The black mind grew from learning and innerstanding the complex African/world landscape. From animals to weather/elements, food and humans, to eventually medicines, seasons, the stars, and so much more.

- African families passed by in peace until things became over populated and in natural creation the black man began to settle issues in exhibition. The competitive nature of the black man in exhibition birth the first sports and martial arts. Once population growth continued, disputes over land and resources became worse sometimes violent. The joining of tribe villages and empires by marriage was a way to expand on resources, land, and stop wars. Some adapted beliefs, others held on to traditional ideologies.

Word passed through storytelling and word of mouth.... until negus started writing. First sand/dirt, themselves, stone/walls, and then paper. Where was first paper/ink made?

- Learning and innerstanding the early Earth and seasons and its effects on the black man and his/her life... That knowledge alone birth many of today's spiritual beliefs and first religions. During this time our mutated (*recessive gene) selves wondered in cold ass Eur-asia. In many places the cold lasts for many many months every year, causing resources to be scarce. When resources are scarce, many things happen to the mind. 1 yo ass is rarely happy, comfortable, and secure. But it's always on the defensive looking for a way to gather more resources to control for survival. The more the better no matter if you needed it or not. Hoarding of resources brought peace of mind because mufuckers never knew how long winter was going to be...at least not at first. In warmth and plentiful resources, babies are

always welcomed and praised. Not when it's cold.
and everything is frozen. With caves getting packed.
Less food for bears/animals/humans in the winter...

- Pregnancy meant an extra mouth to feed, less
traveling possible death for the spouse, which caused many
other complications for survivors. It was very risky. Also,
when resources are scarce even small population increases
caused many deadly disputes. Lack of resources,
accountability, and women also caused cannibalism,
immense homosexuality, inbreeding, and rape. Causing
slowed evolution.

- Trial and error in the cold is harder, takes longer,
and many died in the process. In the cold, with cold water
and few ways to get warm/dry. How/when do you wash
your ass? Sickness...All the medicines to help you are
frozen and covered in snow...sickness.

- The damp muddy cold weather was a breeding
ground for disease and primal thought. Medieval times
(and many eras before and after) where despicably
trifling and filled with squalor. What was taken, stolen,

burned, each time Africa was invaded? Libraries, temples, lineages of royalty....

- Why they mad? If I was in the cold for years then got to Africa and seen all these beautiful women and men in year round wonderful as weather with all these nice as resources and cold as dance moves ...would I feel some type of way? Only if I was a bitch...and my women wanted to stay with them negus, and the native women didn't want my monkey ass. I can see how you can be mad ...not.

- Black people are vengeful, White people are hateful All want peace of mind. Just don't know how to gain it righteously.

- When the original man dies, so will the Earth.

Azzi Diary Entry #613

For the People for the Future

❖ In celebration of the People, Peace, Unity, harvest, and new Prosperous St. Louis future. On the 5th day

of fall, and the 5th moon before the last day of
spring. Twice a year for 27 hours, Native St. Louisians,
no matter where you are, who you are, who you're
with, or how you feel, you have to smile, bow and/or
hug every stranger/friend/family/foe you cross
paths with. And say "I come in peace" perform a
tumbling routine/physical talent. To showcase your
talent, strength and health to your native kinfolk.

❖ Sing or play an instrument your best 1min
demonstration. Or you could simply bow and hug.

❖ Then say "I leave in peace." (*If a person is too
far away, just yell "Fam Laaay!!") Start a convo with
"Salamu" or don't start a convo and say "I leave in
peace" and/or "may peace be with you", (*and mean
It) and everyone mind their positive peaceful
business. Later have a block party feast. With your
harvest or famous dish. Barbecue fish and

vegetables...fruit contest. It'll be dope because I will only eat fish a few times a year. It will come from the best black fishermen/ farmers/herders.

 ❖ Everything tested for purity.

 ❖ How could we clean the Mississippi and make the fish healthier to eat?

Selah Journal Entry #86

Syr is cool but,

If I could control it, I would have my children wait until mastery of a skill/trade and at the age of 23 before intercourse. -they must be courted for 11months.

 • Music should never promote struggle, mental physical or spiritual negligence. Only stories of how messed up the past was (*learning from it) and how fun, peaceful prosperous, the future will be.

 • If there is a genre that does promote violence, drugs, disrespect, etc...dont call it rap or hip hop.

 • We must control the beat of the drum...

The Fraternity for all Fraternities, The Sorority for all Sororities......The Peoples Union!

Riddle Me This

If you had the opportunity, what would you create to unify the people of this country? Of the world?

_____

_____

_____

_____

_____

_____

_____

_____

_____

_____

_____

_____

_____

_____

_____

_____

_____

_____

_____

_____

_____

_____

_____

_____

_____

_____

If you could join the People's Union, what role would you play in helping it thrive?

_____

_____

_____

_____

_____

_____

_____

_____

_____

_____

_____

_____

_____

_____

_____

_____

_____

_____

_____

_____

_____

_____

_____

_____

_____

_____

_____

_____

Let's think. What do you think the next 50 years will be like for PoC?

What books would you pass along to future generations?

_____

_____

_____

_____

_____

_____

_____

_____

_____

_____

_____

_____

_____

_____

_____

_____

_____

_____

_____

_____

_____

_____

_____

_____

_____

_____

_____

_____

_____

_____

If you were in power would you criminalize your own? Why or why not?

What are the pros and cons of criminalizing the very people that were
meant to protect and serve?

_____

_____

_____

_____

_____

_____

_____

_____

_____

_____

_____

_____

_____

_____

_____

_____

_____

_____

_____

_____

_____

_____

_____

_____

_____

_____

_____

_____

Do you believe this country/Government wants the best for all its citizens? Why or why not?

_____

_____

_____

_____

_____

_____

_____

_____

_____

_____

_____

_____

_____

_____

_____

_____

_____

_____

_____

_____

_____

_____

_____

_____

_____

_____

_____

List 5 essential resources you need to survive.

_____

_____

_____

_____

_____

_____

_____

_____

_____

_____

_____

_____

_____

_____

_____

_____

_____

_____

_____

_____

_____

_____

_____

_____

_____

Do you like the current state of your community? What are you willing to do to make it better for everyone?

_____

_____

_____

_____

_____

_____

_____

_____

_____

_____

_____

_____

_____

_____

_____

_____

_____

_____

_____

_____

_____

_____

_____

_____

Let's think. Are your beliefs based off fear? What are your beliefs based on?

_____

_____

_____

_____

_____

_____

_____

_____

_____

_____

_____

_____

_____

_____

_____

_____

_____

_____

_____

_____

_____

_____

_____

_____

_____

_____

_____

_____

Ask yourself, do my beliefs oppress others? Do they cause others to hate or do negative things? If so, why?

What would you be doing if you no longer had to work?

List 10 rules of life, you believe, everyone should live by. Do you live by them? How has it helped you? How has it helped others?

_____

_____

_____

_____

_____

_____

_____

_____

_____

_____

_____

_____

_____

_____

_____

_____

_____

_____

_____

_____

_____

_____

_____

_____

_____

What makes you proud of your culture? What disappoints you?

How can you bring the best out of those around you?

_____
_____
_____
_____
_____
_____
_____
_____
_____
_____
_____
_____
_____
_____
_____
_____
_____
_____
_____
_____
_____
_____
_____
_____
_____
_____
_____
_____

What are 20 things every kid should know by the age of 16?

What are 20 things every man should know by the age of 25?

_____

_____

_____

_____

_____

_____

_____

_____

_____

_____

_____

_____

_____

_____

_____

_____

_____

_____

_____

_____

_____

_____

_____

_____

_____

_____

What is your personal definition of freedom?

List 10 things that make you cry or smile at today's world.

_____
_____
_____
_____
_____
_____
_____
_____
_____
_____
_____
_____
_____
_____
_____
_____
_____
_____
_____
_____
_____
_____
_____
_____
_____
_____
_____
_____

Lets think, outside of race and religion. How can you seperate a large group of people? Example: Credit Score, Criminal Record...etc? Please explain in detail.

What forms of education do you believe are best for our youth?

_____

_____

_____

_____

_____

_____

_____

_____

_____

_____

_____

_____

_____

_____

_____

_____

_____

_____

_____

_____

_____

_____

_____

_____

_____

_____

_____

_____

In what era of American History have the descendants of Africa been treated with equality? Let's think, why would that be.

Think of someone you don't like. What/Who, taught you to hate or feel some type away towards a group of humans of a different color? Background? Belief? Personal experiences? Please explain.

How would you feel in a nation controlled by Blacks? Black Cops? Black Elected officials? Black Media? Black Holidays? Black Foreign Affairs? Etc. Do you think it would be successful? What would make it successful? What would stop it from being successful?

What's the difference between hip hop and rap?

_____

_____

_____

_____

_____

_____

_____

_____

_____

_____

_____

_____

_____

_____

_____

_____

_____

_____

_____

_____

_____

_____

_____

_____

_____

_____

_____

_____

Who would you classify under hiphop/rap?

Is silence in the mist of oppression, betrayal or self-perservation?

What is the human purpose on Earth? To help the Earth live? Or to help the Earth die? How can we unify in this purpose?

Dedication

To the righteous women, men, and children with St. Louis in their veins and warmth in their hearts. May peace be forever with you. Live long and prosper! The Good must UNITE!!!!

To the mighty ATG
May the sun always shine on you and your scenery is flooded with geniune smiles, wealth, and well wishes.

To SMD
Thank you for being my Peace and grease in the mist of chaos and dryness.